# CHRIST NEVER SHOWED UP!

*the disappointing near-death of Joe McPuppet and his curious life afterward*

TIM KIRK

Artwork by Alejandra Fernandez and Mark Givens

*CHRIST NEVER SHOWED UP!*
*the disappointing near-death of Joe McPuppet and his curious life afterward*
by Tim Kirk

ISBN: 978-1-949790-56-6
eISBN: 978-1-949790-57-3



Artwork by Alejandra Fernandez, Mark Givens, and Tim Kirk
Layout and book design by Mark Givens
Richard J's puppet plays used by kind permission of Joel Huschle
Joe's handwriting is based on a typeface by Afiq Anggriawan, modified and expanded by Mark Givens.

First Pelekinesis Printing 2022

For information: Pelekinesis, 112 Harvard Ave #65, Claremont, CA 91711 USA

Library of Congress Cataloging-in-Publication Data

Names: Kirk, Tim (Film producer), author. | Fernandez, Alejandra (Artist), artist. | Givens, Mark, artist.
Title: Christ never showed up : the disappointing near-death of Joe McPuppet and his curious life afterward / Tim Kirk ; artwork by Alejandra Fernandez ; artwork by Alejandra Fernandez and Mark Givens.
Description: Claremont, CA : Pelekinesis, [2022]
Identifiers: LCCN 2021038372 (print) | LCCN 2021038373 (ebook) | ISBN 9781949790566 (paperback) | ISBN 9781949790573 (epub)
Subjects: LCGFT: Humorous fiction. | Novels.
Classification: LCC PS3611.I752 C47 2022 (print) | LCC PS3611.I752 (ebook) | DDC 813/.6--dc23
LC record available at https://lccn.loc.gov/2021038372
LC ebook record available at https://lccn.loc.gov/2021038373

www.pelekinesis.com

For Jimmy Caan

For Jimmy Caan

# Diary

I am Joe! I'm turned 16 today This is my diary and only I am writing it.

WHY SHOULD I READ THIS? you asking Joe.

Well How about this: I survived a NEAR DEATH EXPERIENCE. They took my brain out of my body and I was dead! Officially Joe is DEAD! I saw this LIGHT! and I go to a wonderful place and I Saw many of the people Joe love so happy to see again, There is: Spot and Rover, and my little kitty Penny and there is friend Billy and Joe Gramma.

But who WHO is missing? Could it be Jesus who →

FAILED TO SHOW UP!

## June16

Let's go back to the beginning, people. I have never hated anyone when I was in the womb of the mother. I was just a freely peacful person who didn't have a care in teh world, what did I know about a World! I was a baby!

I imagine I would sit and wonder and ponder the univerise and have fun with my little body and who's looking so what's the harM?

THen I'm here and I GO TO CHURCH

Where I learn to believe in a LIE! Now I know about the lie. It is a LIE!!

Hint:: have something to do with fella initials are JC

So here is where Joe live,. And here is Joe walking down street. HE going here. He going there. Everyone say "where you going, Joe?" and they saying "God Bless you!" HOW can people say?

I was DEAD! I saw the light and heard the trumpets...Time for Jesus to enter. To receive he faithful servant → Joe. 'Where is he", the stagehands whisper, the audiance waits, I'M SERIOUSLY DYING, and no show from the primadonna! Sticke up the band and turn on the houselights people cuz JESUS HAS LEFT THE BUILDING!

People on streewt don't know that. They only know old Joe. The Joe they know - he be happy and shout "God Blees you too!" right back or even say it first!

When I home - there is Mirror! Joe get it. Joe is changed. He always big . Associate Pastor Stephen he always calling Joe "Big Joe" after communion. But New Joe not smiling all the time. He head is shaved and they make stitches out of metal now and they are there. In Joe Head.

So not they people fault. Underneath everything they do and all they smiles Joe can tell. They scared of Joe!

## June 17

This from my dummy friend Michael who has a cool brother named Richard J To be clear: Richard J is older brother and is cool. Michael is not.

Don't worry, Joe. Waiting for salvation is like waiting on a package in the mail. Just when you think it's never coming, Jesus shows up.

Get well soon. God Bless you.

Michael

Nice try dummy Michael! I wasn't WAITING, I was THERE!

So here is a message to all of you who thinkign that the Rapture is Coming →
You know the story: First there is Rapture and all Good Christians fly up to heaven. And then it's hell on earth, biblical Apocaplyse! This all true.

Next part → after years of Tribulations, Jesus Comes and saves everyone who is left on Earth! RIght? RiGHT!?

WRONG?! Jesus will be in Heaven's alley blowing bubbles and swatting with he hand! Or humming loudly in movie theater and annoying to all that hear.

Guess who listening to you when you pray Michael? When you clasp hands on your knees and prary, "Dear Jesus, now I lay me down to sleep. Pray the Lord my soul to keep..." Good LUCK! He's not listening.

I'm Joe! I've been to the place where Jesus would answer your prayer calls if he felt like it, but DON'T HOLD YOUR breaTH!

Right before the operation, on my BRAIN, Old Joe and friend Gabriel are in the hospital room. He friend older than Joe = is Gabriel. He get down on knee because Joe cannot: Joe is strapped to gurney: only fingers free so Gabriel stick Old Joe favorite bible in his hand.

Then: Gabriel start to pray and Joe saying "amen" "amen" over and over.

Here what Gabriel pray: "Oh Jesus Christ, our Lord and Savior, we pray for our brother Joe McClain in your holy name. Please watch over Joe in this difficult time. If, in you infinite wisdom, it is Joe's time to come home, please receive your faithful servant, Oh Lord, and welecome him to his eternal reward so that he can live for eternity in your loving embrace."

And then Joe Die and what happen?

You KNOW WHAT HAPPEN. I got there but where is Jesus? He blow me off!

I feel for all the good people. The soldier on the battlefeild, who praying "dear Lord, please protect me" he say but ZZZZZ (Jesus is takin a nap right now call back later).

There the doctor in the operating room " Jesus, guide my hand" (Jesus has other plans right now SORRY!)

A Mother who love her son Joe so much and want him to love Jesus like he used to – Old Joe love Jesus he whole life! She on knees by Joe bed in recovery room. Praying. Praying. "SHHH, Mama. Don't bother Jesus right now he taking a long bubble bath."

## Sunday

It is first Sunday since I out of Hospital. No way Joe going to Church no matter whaat he Mom say Michael say!

Joe take a hike. He up top of hill: is tallest in whole town. He look at his world, look down on JOE LITTLE WORLD.

There it is. All below him. The church and all of it. Joe is on this very hill every year at Easter – Is blowing the trumpet for "blast of trumpet" part in Easter Pageant. Right when Jesus roll away stone and come back. Triumphant horn

Now Joe know real story of Easter. JC been snoozing in the cave 3 days and now he just heading home for some pizza and more ZZZs. Don't wake.

Can't bother to come and welcome he good friend Joe at Gates of Heaven.

Joe spend every moment of life here. Go to Church. Babtize in Church. Play on cHurch playground. Joe school is not City school, is Church school all the way to senior year. He sing in Choir. He write Puppet plays and he perform Puppet play for all the little kids so they can grow up to love Jesus like Old Joe love Jesus.

Joe know now he was played. Joe is the puppet! My new name –

# Joe McPuppet!

June 22

Behold behold!! Joe former life

# Featherville First Baptist

*Jim's Corner*

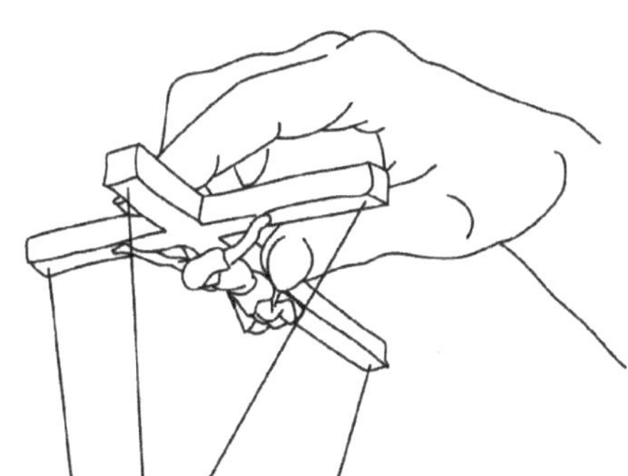

**Dear Members of The Congregation,**

It's your old friend, Pastor Jim, with his monthly update on our Puppet Ministry!

It's that time of year again, folks. Time to make sure our puppets are looking their best (no hanging threads or sagging stuffing). Time to re-paint those backdrops and re-tune the the CD-player. And time to make sure our MESSAGE is straight, is clean and is ready to go!

Yes, it is Easter, and many a Christian puppeteer is having a sleepless night! But the Puppet Crew from classroom B are up to the task! Joe McClain has written a doozy of a puppet play for the Easter service, one that will lift your heart and your soul in rejoicing in His name.

Will they be ready? Well, my adoptive son, Jim Jr (Carl) and the rest of our steady puppeteers are practicing day and night. It's hard work but, oh, so rewarding. Let us remember that we are anointed for a reason. To Praise The Lord! With every tool that he gives us, we must Praise The Lord!

1 Praise ye the LORD.

Praise God in his sanctuary:
praise him in the firmament of his power.

2 Praise him for his mighty acts:

praise him according to his excellent greatness.

3 Praise him with the sound of the trumpet:

praise him with the psaltery and harp.

4 Praise him with the timbrel and dance:

praise him with stringed instruments and organs.

5 Praise him upon the loud cymbals:

praise him upon the high sounding cymbals.

6 Let every thing that hath breath praise the LORD.

Praise ye the LORD.

- The Psalms 150 (KJV)

Praise him even with **Puppets?** Yes! Praise ye The Lord! May God bless you and keep you well in this most glorious of His seasons.

Jim Hill

Pastor Jim Hill

Featherville First Baptist. 117 E. Springfield Road, Featherville, Idaho.

**June 23**

Here the proof, friends of Joe. Read please:

# Patient Treatment Form

Patient Name: *Joe McClain* Date of Birth: *6/15/2005*
Height: *6' 2''* Weight: *180 lbs.* Phone No.: *(702) 381-2456*
Address:
Reason for Admittance: *Cranial Injury*

Diagnosis at Admittance: *Tumor was discovered when patient was in the hospital for unrelated cranial injury on 5/13/2021 Attending physicians deemed tumor as massive and malignant. Tests indicated that it was life-threatening. Emergency surgery was performed on 5/21/2021*

*Patient flatlined at 10:07:00 and revived at 10:08:51.*

Date Discharged: Physician Approved? ❑ Yes ☒ No
Reason for Discharge: ❑ Patient Deceased ❑ Patient Transferred ☒ Patient Terminated w/o Approval
Diagnosis at Discharge:

*Patient has recovered motor skills and most brain functions. However, tests have shown that, while motor skills seem unaffected, his brain activity is compromised. Mainly thought processes and patterns...*

*...language skills and structure effected...*

*...cognitive connective tissues disturbed...*

*Final analysis: Patient appears resistant to further tests or procedures. Without sufficient follow up, my professional opinion is that patient's condition may deteriorate. Possible outcomes are: decreased mental ability, paralysis or death.*

Lorens
Signature

06/02/2021
Date

## June 25

Who are you? Who is reading this? What you thinking of you friend Joe?
Maybe you thinking:
**"I GUess you hate God too, right Joe?"**
Guess again, dear reader. MY BEEF IS NOT WITH HIM!

"And God so loved the world that he gave his only son..." Thank, but no THANKS!
God promise that Jesus love and protect us. Well, where was he when I cruised by the Pearly Gates?
Hey JC, I got some news for you. You just made your father a liar.
How that feel?
You made GOD a liar!

## Is another Sunday

Joe not going anywhere near church now! Big problem for Joe Mom. Her name is now Mama McPuppet! You like it? She is not liking new Joe. She want me back at church. "Everybody mis you!"
She bring me this. It is from Pastor Jim. He like a bear with glasses on. Gentle and smiling most. He teach Joe in Sunday School since 5 years old. He the one who get Joe involved in
Puppet Ministry. IDEA is: perform fun plays for kids with puppets AND teach them the Word of God.
Joe is good at this real good. He perform his plays for the Sunday school – ALL classes – ALL age groups – and TWO times a year in Main Church.
ALSO! BIG DEAL! Is that Joe perform every year for SteadyFaith Church for World Revival weekend! That the big mega church and maybe 2,000 people see Joe and he puppets.
YAWN and WHO CARES!

THE KNOW IT ALL

A puppet play by Joe McClain

SETTING: A school classroom. Chalk board in background reads "Histo:

PROPS: ruler, books, cellphone.

CHARACTERS:

Teacher (Mama. Mercy in her pattern dress costume.)
Little Stevie (the Know It All)
Students – 2 or 3 puppets
Hobo Joe
Baby
Jesus

TEACHER: Good morning, class. Today we will continue our review of week's lesson. Who remembers what we discussed?

LITTLE STEVIE: The Prodigal Son!

TEACHER: That is correct, Little Stevie. But please raise your hand when you want to talk.

LITTLE STEVIE: (to audience) I only have two of them!

TEACHER: Who can tell us the story of the Prodigal Son?

LITTLE STEVIE: (raising both hands and waving them around) I do! I do!
(puppet turns to audience)

LITTLE STEVIE: (talking in rushed tone) A rich man gave his son a lot of money. The son goes crazy and spends it all. When he goes home, he tells his dad that he is poor and asks him if can work for him but the father gives him a hug and says, 'Welcome home, son.' The moral is: God will always take you back, no matter what you do.

(Hobo Joe Enters)

Hobo Joe: I heard that. What do you know? You are just a kid?

TEACHER: Well, Hobo Joe, the bible has a story to tell us. (quoting Lucas 18:1-8) "At that time came the disciples unto to Jesus saying, "Who, then, is the greatest in the kingdom of heaven?" And Jesus called a little child unto him, and set him in the midst of them. 3 And he said..."

(enter Jesus)

JESUS: Verily I say unto you, except you be converted and become as little children, you shall not enter the kingdom of heaven.

(enter Baby. Baby moves close to Jesus who hugs him.)

JESUS: Whosoever, therefore, shall humble himself as this little child is the greatest in the kingdom of heaven. And whosoever shall receive one such child in my name receiveth me.

TEACHER: What do you say now, Hobo Joe?

HOBO JOE: Uh, I think I hear my cell phone ringing.
I need to check my twitter. Bye!

LITTLE STEVIE: I guess I really am a Know It All after all!
(Teacher shakes head.) (Curtain.)

Brother in christ,

A big "howdy" and "praise His name" from Pastor Jim. We miss your fellowship here at Sunday worship, and also Wednesday and Friday youth groups.

We miss your strong faith, and your humor and smile (that big Joe Mclain Smile!).

Please join us soon! Just last Sunday my adoptive son Jim Jr (Carl) asked me, "Where is the funny puppet man?"

Yours in the Lord, your pal,

Jim Hill

PS. Here is a copy of your play "The Know It All" which we performed at the Summer Daze Retreat last week. You write so well!

Thank you thank you! And this was indeed a good play and I wrote manny more but did it matter when I was dead? → no!

YES: I saw the light.

NO: I did not see Jesus!

WHY: BECAUSE HE NEVER SHOWED UP!

Now you you know why I am angry!

## June 28

Joe look around today and he decide. This no place for Joe no more. So he say: **SIN CITY, HERE HE COME!**

In church. In movies. in Youth Group. They TELL Joe, again and again: "Sin! Sin is in City! You know what City is worst, Joe? The worst city: IS LOS ANGELES!"

"A wicked place, young Joe. A wicked wicked place filled with doomed and wicked persons."

sound like place for Joe!

## June 29

First stop is BANK.

Some guy outside is freaked out and scream: "the machine eat his card!"

Joe is staring at him, jus watchin the guy freaking out. DUDE IS soooooooooooo frusttrarted, sssssssssssooooo DISappointed!

HEy mister, Joe know a little bit about DISAPPOINTMENT!

Joe tell Teller: "Withdraw all, pleaze!" Is all money in Joe World. Is money saved for mission work! HA! Now Joe has a real mission! (Winking)

Next stop: Post office. I said, "Post Office, the only way I want my mail delivered is Jesus Christ brings it hisself" and they laughed. I laughed right along

because they GET IT! JC SUPERSLUG wouldn't get off his butt long enough to say "Hey Joe, welcome to Heaven." SO how is he going to find the energy to deliver Joe Mail? IF he even awake!

Wind your clock, Jesus, just once!

from Joe backyrad

# July 2!!

Joe in seat 5C on Greyhound bus! Hollywood bound!

Feeling is happy! Feeling is sad

Feeling is familiar to previous experience: leaving LIFe for Next place, in Heavan.

He happy and sad then too, but you know all about that.

This time will be different: Joe sure that this trip will be different: There will be no big Let Down in Sin City!

Joe figures that LA Sin City is one place that Jesus won't go.

That okay with Joe.

IT all going away outside Joe window There goes the DMV where Joe get license.

There is neighborhood he knock on doors for Sucker Christ.

There go High School he never go to. Kids playing soccer - what that like?

To pass the time, I am PLayhing a game with JC: we argue. Go like this:

JC: "Say dear Joe, you recalling this store? Mrs Mom bought you bike."

ME: "What you care, Looser!?!"

Joe always win - have much fun!

There a sign reading: Leavin "Featherville."

Joe never been this far.

Greetings Joe,

It's your old Pastor Jim again with some reading for your trip. Your mother tells me that you feel this journey is part of God's plan for you.

I wish you God speed and hope that, as you travel, you will keep in mind all that you have learned here at Featherville First Baptist.

You have often assisted me in Sunday School 2 with our class lesson about trash. Remember how it goes? You would lead the class by saying "We all throw trash away. But what do we NEVER throw away?" And the class would make their own lists and share later?

Here is your pal Pastor Jim's list:

Keep your Faith

Keep your Love of God

Keep your fellowship those that are close to you in God's love ~ Michael, Gabriel, Jim Jr (Carl), the members of Team Puppet.

And remember always, "Jesus said, Suffer little children, and forbid them not, to come unto me: for of such is the kingdom of heaven." Lucas 19:14.

Jim Hill

## July 3

Still ON BUS still NOT THERE!

No one is waiting for Joe. But there is someone he want to see. Is Richard J! Richard J is older brother of Joe dumb friend Michael (dummy) Joe know Richard J forever. Joe Look up at him when Richard J was Pastor Jim's assistant (long before it Joe job). He apple of Pastor Jim eye. Very good kid and beloved by church.

But Richard J figure it out before Joe. Then he Good Kid no more. Bad. Bad! Then VERY bad! and then gone.

Joe MCP kinda guy! A hero.

## July 5

**SIN CITY** is a **Let DOWN**!

The stories Joe was told in sermons. The little book Chick Tracts cartoons he pass out at mall - more lies?

Where is Hooker in mini skirt? Where Satanist in black hood? Where the gay rapist with the leather pants and all that hair?

Sixth street in Los Angeles. Just poor people.

**Now on ANOTHER BUS**. Now riding to Richard J address. Homeless guy (hobo?) he help Joe get on the right bus IN EXCHANGE Hobo want to look inside Joe brain. Look at he gash and the stitches. Inside Joe Brain.

"Move on in! Plenty room! Staay awhile!"

Now is LATER: it is right address for Richard J but Richard J is not here. It a dump. A house. Very dirty and no lights working. No one home Mattress on floor so Joe sleep here. IN LA!

Nighty night

**But** NO SLEEP

Joe looking at broken window Stain down wall. Rain?

He remembers Richard J room at he parent house. It a lot like Joe room. Neat and nice. Picture of Jesus over b ed.

Joe look again at broeken window At dirty walls.

Then Joe Happy: Richard J made it OUT!

## July 6

Today I meeting many of Richard J friends. They coming and going. This is how Joe learns that Richard J is in jail.

They are coming to pick up stuff Richard J borrowed from them. Richard J has very good friends who would lend himn a color TV a game machine a lpad. Most of clothes. They lend him really all Richard J have! So many friends! And this is how Joe learn Richard J in Corcoran State Prison.

## July 7

Bus Again. Headed north. CORCORCAN BOUND!

JC: "Say old boy Joe old friend, you ever think that Richard J don't know you are coming, maybe don't even remember you, little Joe McClain from church, friend of brother Michael?"

ME: Shut up, you slacker and you wrong!"

Joe win again

## Saturday

Here is Joe in the "Big house" (prison.) How he get in ther? Joe plays the game of being Old Joe. "I bring message of hope to lost brother of God, our dear brethren of Featherville First Baptist who was save and wash in blood of Lamb, our lLOrd Jsus Christ.............

It hurt! It hurt NEW joe! But it work and here Joe is in white room with glass window waiting for Richard J and HERE he is!!!

## July 9

Rolling down Freeway number 5. What a trip! Richard J looking good. Many tatoos and not one a Crucifix. He a man of mystery He put on show for prison people "He not know Joe." (Wink wink.) He saying "who fuck you?" and "what fuck want?"

Then he "remember" and full of complitments for New Joe. Proud of him considers him very close friend. How Joe tell this? Richard J describe all tht was lame about Old Joe. He a "looser" and " a Mama boy" HE believe all crap told him and kiss Pastor Jim fat behind to get to God Quicker.

Joe get it, Richard J! You talking in code. We on same frequency

Then here comes Richard J with the directions for Joe:

1) "go write another puppet play" (Joe on iT!)

2) "don come back." Joe never going back home to Featherville, so worry not Richard j

And 3) wich is hard to understand at first so Richard J say it many times. "Go fuck yourself." "go fuck yourself"

What mean?

Then he say "Get lost→!" and Joe smile because he know how to do that.

## July 10

Home of RIchasrd J is locked up. Through window Joe see just pots and pans in pile in livigin room. Joe don't care because Joe know just where to go

So now Joe is **LOST**

It work. Joe does randowm walking plan, turn here, then count 10, then right, then left - not good enough, so make random decisions, like surprise Joe self. Like suddenly run down alley then stop and turn around 3 times and more run.

It work. Here Joe is onn Hollywood Blved. And what is waiting ther for Joe? Why it is a apartement. And guessing what? This place for rent. Big building and many rooms. One for Joe!

Pays cash up front. He low on money but no care! No light. No bed. Bugs and something smeel bad. But Joe take deep breath

Ah! He safe! No way Jesus here

He home

But **NO SLEEp**

Guess who still gets the blues sometimes ? And if'yre guessing it's JOe, well, RIGHT

But WHO Do I Talk to NOW?

I ain't no BUd**dist** - THat Gandi ain't JOe's speed...too skinny!

An I mean, I still believe in GOd, more than ever, because I been to Heaven, I KNOW GOD EXIST. So, no, GOD Is not on my SHIT-LIST! But come on, how do you rspect a guy (GOD) who's still letting his kid live at home, hang out all day no job, nothing to do but greeet peple at the gates of Heaven, and tell them they have ever lasting life

NOTA BAD JOB ← but he blows it off, blows IT OFF → and jus slack off!

I mean, how can YOU hONESTLY pray to the Father of such a person? Call HIm HEAVENLy FAther?

I can't. Keep trying. Ican't.

## July 11

Here it is **HOLLYWOOD AND VINE** -- Another let down, no prostitute no drug. Another lie!!! But lots crzy Lzy people and real crummy shops sell shit. Joe buy sunglasses and a t-shirt say "Budweiser. King of beers.'" Tak that "king of KINGS!"

And crummy electronics place. Joe get first TV. Never watch TV at home - we read Bible verses or "talk as family" AND Joe Ask store owner for VCR. "Why want?: Say tan guy not tan like Jorge who do lawn at Chruch, but tan and little guy (from China?)

"Just want it" say Joe. Joe know about VHS from watching videos at Youth Group.

Tan Guy sell Joe VCR. Tan Guy show Joe box of tapes. Jo look. No movies Joe every hear of. Which is good.

NO "In His Steps"

NO "Amazing Love: The story of Hoseo"

NO "A Theif in the Night"

All NEW movies to Joe. NEW world.

I get one = fat guy hanging onto window with sticky stuff - he looking inside - real funny look on face - maybe pervert?

Joe: I take it.

Guy say: 10 for 1 dollar. No, Joe say - one at a time. Joe take it sloooooooow!

## July 12

THe movie! **"WHERE's HARRY CRUMB"**

Have you seen this Movie!?! It is hilarious and thinks Joe: a Great piece of art.

First real movie for Joe and what a film it is!

It NOT: "Left Behind"

It NOT: Left Behind: Tribulation Force."

It IS: "Where Harry Crumb?"

Turn out that fat guy is detective: he puts on all kind of disguises: everywhere he goes has lots of light and manny pretty people. He got hit on the head and now lives in a wonderful place that looks a lot like plaNet Earth!

Funniest scene? Impossible to pick just one. Here a favorite though:

Harry is dress like crazy cook (master of disguis) and he get propelled through a tube (don ask) and fly through window and land in a guy's chair in that guy living room. In he chair.

And Guy look at Harry Crumb and Harry Crumb say:

HARRY CRUMB: "I meant to do that"

**Great movie. And a manny laaughs too. JOe sez: Check it out!**

BLOCKBUSTER
WHO'S
HARRY
99¢

"Life Sentence"
A puppet play by Joe McPuppet

Set is prison.

Prisoner #1: Let me out of prison! I want out of here!

Prisoner 2: Not me.

Prisoner #1: You don't want out of prison?

Prison 2 (Rirchard J): No. I have life sentence. Only way out is Death.

Prisoner #1: But there is a real escape, right Pastor Jim?

Pastor Jim: Yes, Richard J. The bible tells us all about it. It is called The Great Escape.

Richard J: The "great Escape" is to die and go to Heaven. No way!

Prisoner 1 and Pastor Jim: (at same time) You don't want to go to Heaven?!!

Richard J: No, I have a friend who has been there and he says It is terrible. Jesus doesn't even show up. Ain't that right, Joe?

Joe: It sure is!

THE END

It return to Joe but happy Richard J read it first. Joe bet he get big laugh and be impressed. too

## July 23

Joe was sitting in the lobby of he building, the place he live, not really waiting just hanging out. MAYBE waiting. What for?

The phone there ring. FIRST time Joe is hearing it Ringing. No one answer phone because no one there in the room. It empty room so Joe answer. Conversation go like this:

GO like this:

Joe: What?

Phone: Who isi this?

Joe: My name is Joe! WHo this?

Phone: My name is Patrick. I want to buy your car.

Joe : What car?

Patrick: Your 87 Civic.

JOE: Patrick!! I do not have a car for sale. Goodbye and neveR call again.

END OF CALL

Joe o n the Couch now: jus thinking , don't even remember about what - is not about bag on floor -that is where he keep the Fat boy movie in there, jus thining Thinking...

Wait! JOE looks at the New Phone! IN Joe Rooooooom! How did it get there?

Then Joe remember telephone Guy put it there. Joe pay him to put it. BUT

HOW did JOE answer THIS phone in LOBY? A vision? A illusion? Tricks like on Candy Camera?

**Answer is no!**

**A Messsage! And Joe reciceves it loud and clear!**

LOUD AND CLEAR, RICHARD J! Joe Goes Shopping for a car tomorrow! And Joe knows already which one he wants

## July 24

I FOUND IT!

To Place Your FREE Ad* Call 800-300-2777
Or Visit www.recycler.com Hablamos Español

ALSO FOLLOW US ON

**FOR SALE**
**1987 CIVIC**

It runs.
Some new parts. Cheap.

$800.00 obo

# HUNDREDS OF USED CARS FOR SALE EVERY WEEK

*Some categories excluded (please call for details)

One 87 Civic !!!!

Not as EaSY to find as you'd Think! BUt I GOT it, RIchard J! REqusting furthR insturCtions!

## July 27

Joe head keep slipping and not remembering, but he knows one thing: he know he **HEAD HURTS!**

Joe can't move. Joe can't sleep. Joe can't even watch VHS tape. Oh that John Candy Better not thingk of that – Laughing hurt Joe HEAD!

Here Joe Mom. Is Mama McPuppet now Joe miss her. Sometimes. but no her dolls!

## July 30

I tell you now about:

### JOE VISIT DOCTOR pLACE

It Hospital. Joe walks in . They very worried. Everyboddy worried. Stitches look bad are bad. "Joe must stay over night!" Joe say no, no no, no! "You need Medicine" "Joe take medicine!"

They only let go if promise to go to something called Grief Group. It is like place you talk, "talk with others" say big DOCTor. He give Joe a card. Joe say Yes, syes, yes so they clean he head and let go.

Some pills - not work so hot. Make Joe sick in stomach.

## AUGUst

And now Joe is reporting on the place that is GRIEF GROUP OOOOOH GOD!

This was worse than the new pills.

Setting: White room, green walls, chairs in a circle, 8 people and councelor. AN JOE!

We take turns being SPEAKER. Say name and be → SPEAKER

Believe It: every one of these people has lost "someone Dear."

Believe it: Each one had a "Visitation". Yep, their dead Dear came back for visit! Guess what the Dead One have to sAy: Each one say: "You are SOOO Wonderful and God appreciates all that you have done. Heaven is wondderful and I waiting here for you." Joe like: Whaaaaa?

IN other words; THEY LIE!

Guess what: There one SPEAKER who say he been to BOTH places. He big shot.

He say name and stand up and BIG SHOT say: "I been to both Heaven

and Hell." Report from Big Shot: "I preferred Heaven."
People like that! Big shot with smile is smug smile

**Get the picture, you DUmB Shits: It's The Same place!**

Only one who not talk (be SPEAKER) is pretty girl. She wearing black hair and black clothes. Her eyes very big: even bigger with black make up on them. Want a secret? Joe folloe her! And that is how he discover

**GOTHS!**

Joe driving Civic 87 and she walking. Is tough to follow her. Eventuallly she go through big iron Gate and up hill. Lots of hills, all very grassy: is like a park. Joe have to look hard but there are white rocks. They flat so not rocks but headstones. IS Cemetery! Except headstones don't stand up - they lying don on earth. Is special kind of cemetery Joe ask guy there → he with rake → he say: "Is Forest Lawn Memorial Park" and "is Special Place" and "look around. NO headstones to see. Only pleasant green hills, rolling green hills of Peace." Look around he say Joe look and then he see them:
GOTHS!

## August 2

So here's the letters JOe's getting now:

First from old friend Michael (dummy) writes "Hey Joe it's Michael and we miss you at Prayer group. I miss your fellowship and your friend ship. I know that Gabriel, Pastor Jim, Jim Jr (Carl) and your mom are missing you too. Please come home and let God back into your heart."

IS ALL like thi:

From Pastor Jim: blah blah. Joe answer: sorry but JC is a couch-potato and not worth you love.

From Mama McPuppet: blah blah. Joe answer: sorry mom but Jesus suck the bong long and hard.

Little Joey: Daddy I miss you
HA HA, that Joe little joke. Never forget Joe sense of humor – he get you everytime!

## August 4

Yes, today after Group – Joe went home to place and put on new shirt (Budwieser King of Beers) and he go straight to Forest Lawn. There they is: GOTHS.

Joe just walk right up: "Hello. Joe McPuppet here!"

Eye opening evening!!! Joe has never been around a group of people like these, Damn Good times!

Here's the thing: These people "Goths" are much like JOe! We get along great. Laugh and smoke a clove cigarette. BEST ParT: They hate Jesus just like Joe! That's a THUMBS UP!

THumbs DOWN is they **don't** BELIEVE in JEsus!

They don't believe in him and they hate him!?! JOe confused.

Still, Goth rules in perpetuitty! But still a little lame. What Joe hates is real.

## August 6

Guess who I hung out with again today? THE GOTHS!

YEah, today a field trip with Goths: The Masoleum. IS a big big huge stone building in middle of park. Is a walk up hill from behind Little Church where usual hang. So, we call it "Field trip" and laugh as we do.

Inside MAsoleum is hall and halls. Is locked but Joe friends know way Long halls and on each wall one can find a big square or two. These Drawers! Inside drawers = the Dead!!!

The goths all havin fun, hanging out with they phones and modeling for their grave sites and

Lie down on marble floor. They act Like it's their fifnal resting palce. MAYBE FOR THEM, but JOe knows eternity He's seen it. This CAn't be undone for poor Joe,

Let us imagine dear Joe is dead: I'll be in Heaven, but alwayS on the look out because Joe always gettin the DODGE from the loser Son of MAN.

Picture this: Joe in the clouds or something, Joe look around and there'll be Jesus ducking behind another cloud, hiddng behind his golden Crown or something.

OR Joe is waiting in line for some HAPPY thing or another like we do in Heaven and then Joe hear: "There is he is! There is Jesus" someone saying.

But Joe look and is a joke: Sure enough, JC on his Holy Couch zzzz

OR Joe a party for Hommer or Aristotles or someone and there a buzz "guess who coming? Is Jesus." "Jesus on way he coming for sure." And Jackie Gleason and Walt Disney talk like just assume all have "Personal relationship" with Jesus and he come by they parties all the time, "just you wait."

But Midnigh come and DING DONG -- it another no show by Sucker Messiah! However, everybody else there just HAPPY HAPPY anyway and Joe is STUCK in this "heaven!"!!!!!

Back to Goths. Time is now and place is Forest Lawn is special Cemetery The pretty girl and Goths are outside now having fun lying on graves with arms crossed, pertend they dead.

And Joe make a decision which is fuck this world too

I think I'll start burnin shit soon

## Thursday

Joe's Weak. More doctor and more pills and "go to Grief Group. Go to Group!" Instead Joe go to Forest Lawn special cemetary

You see: Joe has been thinking about he many trips to Forest Lawn - to that Cemetery Joe especially thinking about GOTHS and how they love it, they LOVE IT!!

Thy LOVE this cemetery! This place ON EARTH. THeir final RESTING place.

Did you get that part: TO REST! ON EARTH!

This idea? TO REST! ON EARTH! ON THIS VERY PLANET! What a dream. Nowhere else to go , no Holy Jerk-off waiting just to blow you off and never show up.
No ideals shattered, not to have to look back at EVERYONE in your life who was a good Christin like you (Joe was a very good Christian) and think about them: they dummies and fools!
Not have to watch the PICTURE SHOW they show you in Heaven, where you see all you friends and you being good Chrsistains. And thinking to self "Damn, Joe, you were lied to. Them friends is lied to. They Good good people and have no idea what this this Heaven really is. A place where you are blown off repeatedly → blown off for eternity"

I tell you that Idea is tremendously appealing to Joe: To stay on earth for ALL time, and skip this whole Heaven thing forever. Yeah, I'll die, but I won't have to go there. I stay stay stay HERE forever.
So HERE IS THE THOUGHT. Is the fruit of all thinking by your hero, ME, Joe! HEre is The Thought:

Joe build himslef a TEMPLE on this planet Earth! Made by Joe. Joe in the Temple when alive. Joe there when dead. JOe is **ALWAYS** there. Which mean he doesn't have to go to that place he's been (Heaven) and knows how much it hurts.
So, joe make a list:

1) Building a Temple
2) Burning Shit.

3. Greif group.

I'll let you know how it turn out, but I vote YES for 1 and2!

## August 7

Joe's Mind keeps returning again and again to The TEMPLE! He big idea!
It occurs to Joe that somebody somewhere in this Vast History of Time must have thought this up befor Joe: Maybe Joe learn from these:
Let us study:

How about SteadyFaith church? Is a temple? Joe tell you about that already: big super church where Joe perform and thousands pray everyday It built to "honor God" but also tribute to all gGood Christians who pay for it.
A lesson there for Joe?

**Then they is Forest Lawn itself → It was built by a man call himself the BUILDER. He is Hubert Eaton and on a hill one day in 1919 or something - is New Years and he have a vision and he write down he purpose: what kind of cemetery he build: he carve those words in stone: call it Builder Creed: here pictures**

THE BUILDER'S CREED
ENCOURAGED BUT CONTROLLED BY ACKNOWLEDGED ARTISTS; A PLACE WHERE THE SORROWING WILL BE SOOTHED AND STRENGTHENED BECAUSE IT WILL BE GOD'S GARDEN. A PLACE THAT SHALL BE PROTECTED BY AN IMMENSE ENDOWMENT CARE FUND, THE PRINCIPAL OF WHICH CAN NEVER BE EXPENDED—ONLY THE INCOME THEREFROM USED TO CARE FOR AND PERPETUATE THIS GARDEN OF MEMORY.
THIS IS THE BUILDER'S DREAM; THIS IS THE BUILDER'S CREED.
The Builder

THE BUILDER'S CREED
BECAUSE THEY DEPICT AN END, NOT A BEGINNING. THEY HAVE
CONSEQUENTLY BECOME UNSIGHTLY STONEYARDS FULL OF IN-
ARTISTIC SYMBOLS AND DEPRESSING CUSTOMS; PLACES THAT
DO NOTHING FOR HUMANITY SAVE A PRACTICAL ACT, AND
THAT NOT WELL.
I THEREFORE PRAYERFULLY RESOLVE ON THIS NEW YEARS
DAY, 1917, THAT I SHALL ENDEAVOR TO BUILD FOREST LAWN
AS DIFFERENT, AS UNLIKE OTHER CEMETERIES AS SUNSHINE IS
UNLIKE DARKNESS, AS ETERNAL LIFE IS UNLIKE DEATH. I SHALL
TRY TO BUILD AT FOREST LAWN A GREAT PARK, DEVOID OF
MISSHAPEN MONUMENTS AND OTHER CUSTOMARY SIGNS OF
EARTHLY DEATH, BUT FILLED WITH TOWERING TREES, SWEEPING
LAWNS, SPLASHING FOUNTAINS, SINGING BIRDS, BEAUTIFUL STATUARY,
CHEERFUL FLOWERS, NOBLE MEMORIAL ARCHITECTURE WITH
INTERIORS FULL OF LIGHT AND COLOR, AND REDOLENT OF THE
WORLD'S BEST HISTORY AND ROMANCES.
I BELIEVE THESE THINGS EDUCATE AND UPLIFT A COMMUNITY.
FOREST LAWN SHALL BECOME A PLACE WHERE LOVERS NEW
AND OLD SHALL LOVE TO STROLL AND WATCH THE SUNSETS
GLOW, PLANNING FOR THE FUTURE OR REMINISCING OF THE PAST;
A PLACE WHERE ARTISTS STUDY AND SKETCH; WHERE SCHOOL
TEACHERS BRING HAPPY CHILDREN TO SEE THE THINGS THEY READ
OF IN BOOKS, WHERE LITTLE CHURCHES INVITE, TRIUMPHANT
IN THE KNOWLEDGE THAT FROM THEIR PULPITS ONLY WORDS
OF LOVE CAN BE SPOKEN; WHERE MEMORIALIZATION OF LOVED
ONES IN SCULPTURED MARBLE AND PICTORIAL GLASS SHALL BE
ENCOURAGED BUT CONTROLLED BY ACKNOWLEDGED ARTISTS;
A PLACE WHERE THE SORROWING WILL BE SOOTHED AND
STRENGTHENED BECAUSE IT WILL BE GOD'S GARDEN. A PLACE
THAT SHALL BE PROTECTED BY AN IMMENSE ENDOWMENT CARE
FUND, THE PRINCIPAL OF WHICH CAN NEVER BE EXPENDED-ONLY
THE INCOME THEREFROM USED TO CARE FOR AND PERPETUATE
THIS GARDEN OF MEMORY.

What is he saying? : the building of a Memorial is in human nature. Is leaving part of you on Earth. And the bigger the Memorial equals bigger part of You stay on earth

Perhaps Joe learn from this?

How about

PHAROAHS! Probably best builders ever. They build Huge thing: call it Memorial: call it grave: pyramid: it a Temple! So big!

List of problems:

1 – Joe never rich like Pharoahs

#2: Joe has no Money to speak of

Three 3 is this) Joe is Not A CREATIVE TYPE. (Hold applause) (Joe joke) but

seriously New Joe not Creative.

HOW? HOW? HOW?

Joe would pray on it but he know who answers that phone – is Jesus and he won't even pick up! buzz buzz Jesus! Anybody home?!

## August 8

No so much Goths for Joe now But he still go to Forest Lawn Special Place to walk, he walk and he thinkg. What Joe think about? Life mostly Where Joe fit in this world now?

He still **B**elieve but not love what he Believe. He hate it.

Many thoughts for Joe. Oh, goths are here and there. They popping up all the time. But mostly Joe in he own head.

Today is day that Joe hearing **worlds greatest song**! What? Where? Here the scene:

A funeral. Lots of people in black. Joe hanging back/he listening like he do. It on a slope, on a hill on edge of cemetery You can see the grass and stone. You can see neighborhood below - outside of cemetery wall. The Goths who know Forest Lawn Special well: they call that neighborhood "The Avenues." They say gangs live there.

They say that the gang kids get shot dead and buried here on hill because looking down on old neighborhood, they "turf." The Goths at Forest Lawn Special have name for this par of the cemetery: they call it "Gangbanger Alley"

After Preacher talking (while Joe going hmm hmm hmmm not listening)

After done talking, old man stand up. He big and big grey beard - very big man, tattoos all over self. He lift boom box over head and he play World's Greatests Song!

UNFORGIVEN!!! This no kidding Greatest Song of all time! REPEAT: The **greattest Song** of ALL TIME! BY a band called MEtalicA!

what I've felt
what I've known
never shined through in what I've shown
never free
never me
so I dug thee unforgiven

Joe go to baeutiful place. Like living in song. He not know if eyes closed but when song is over, everybody leaving or gone, except old man.

And Joe. Joe have to talk, have to thank him. He talk to old man - he talk about how it means, how much that damn song means to him. Make so much sense. HE talk and talk about how align with he experience - Joe personal experience → he life experience → he afterlife experience.

Joe admit he effusive. He talk a lot.

Old man take a pen and write on paper, and Joe has that paper in hands now It an address to Old man house and Old man has said to come to his house.

What experience. When over – Joe is turning around. Joe turn around. No goths anywhere. Never see again.

## August 9

**THERE'S A MOVIE!!!** Can you believe it?

Joe discover this: Here how happen: Tan Guy say: "there's a movie." Joe is looking around electronic store and I guess talking about Greatest song but not sure he talking out loud.

But Tan Guy (little guy) pull it out of box and hand to Joe. It true! It called "Unforgiven."

**Purchased, yes. TV on, yes.** Ready watch – NOW!

BE KIND
REWIND
THE UNFORGIVEN
Environ 2h 6min
VHS

How did they fuck this up?!

The Unforgiven: The movie

Gimme a break. I mean, this movie seem to have NOTHING to do with the Song "UNForgvinen" which is song they made the movie FROM: yes BASED this movie on the song "Unforgiven" (is by Meatllica) which is the Greatest Song.

And that song is NOT about a COWBOY! Some old guy who is a COWBOY? GET with It:

NOT ABOUT A COWBoy HOLLYWOOD!

*New blood joins this earth*
*and quikly he's subdued*
*through Constant pain disgrace*
*the young boy learns their rules*

**How that about a COWBOY?**

This old Cowboy is weak and weird. Then his mama dies and his little brother and sister are tired so he get some black guy to help him get it on with some whores and then **kill** everyone in the town especially this lame Carpenter or some such who builds houses for everyone and they all have drinks at the SAME bar where he kills them .

I don't expect much from Hollywood, but **C'mon**

## August 10

Joe just visit OLD GUY house. Is walk down street in Avenues. It early morning because Joe can't sleep and nowhere go. Go to Old man house.
He dead. He not there but Joe sees blood in garage when Old wife roll out Taco cart – it cart with grill to make tacos - it wheels go through blood. Old wife say "Suicide" she say "Sad man. Sad man."
Joe sad too. He know the bummer that awaiting man in Heaven. Probably right at exact moment, right now Joe cry a little.
"you take!" She say of old Man – "He want you have it."
So now joe own taco cart.
Joe Pushing away but he stop. More cry So he Say words

*throughout his life the same*
*he's battle constantly*
*this fight he cannot win*
*a tired man he see no longer cares*
*the old man then preparre*
*to die regretfully*
*that old man here is me*

Which is words to Unforgiven. Like a prayer **BUT NOT** a prayer!
Farewell Old man. Ride em Cowboy! Sorry you will not be seeing anyone up there. You share JOE Secreet now

## (many days later)

Sorry no Joe so long. He bveen working! Here the places he seel the tacos: YOUTUBE. Yes, they make little movies here and not far from Joe place. Like blocks away – easy to push the cart. Joe learning on job, maybe Tacos not so good. Youtube not care. They all running around film each other. They eat a taco and maybe they don't like it and film that or

Other One LIKE it and maybe they argue! In a movie!
also WE WORKS. Big building with manny windows. Also not far and Joe buy good ingredients this time. "It all in ingredients" say Joe Gramma (now Gramma McPuppet ha!) (though dead) He also buy hotdogs. Young people like hot dogs.
Young people all work at WE WORKS. They do OWN work, they tell you. "We just rent a space" they tell you. "What a Space" ask Joe.
"A table."

TRaVEL TOWN. This one a hike. It a little park in a big park - which is Griffith Park. Joe hook up taco cart to 87 Civic. That take all day So Joe end up with very little time to sell tacos at travel Town.
It ia place for kids to run around and play on old trains. They mostly nap time when Joe there.
That Okay Joe just sit still and do some thinking.
Thinking PAUL HILTON for some reason. Like a dream of Paul HILTON. He (Paul) is surrouneded by puppets. He is performing at SteadyFaith church - in a bright spotlight, and he is making puppets dance and making puppets talk: They say:
"Oh Adam. I am so happy in the Garden."
"The Lord make it for us, indeed. It is Eden."
"Oh Adam, I long to eat that red apple."
"No Eve. It is forbidden by GOD!"

Which is actual puppet play that written by and performed by Paul Hilton in that very church several years ago. Joe was there. It a big hit and maybe get more "Amens" than Joe own work, Joe own puppet plays he perform there at SteadyFaith.
Paul do his trademark bow after performance: he clasp hands in prayer then

swing all way above head then down to floor in deep bow

In Joe thoughts - Joe is remember how he feeling ANGER and ENVY for Paul Hilton an d he success - and how he feeling BAD for feeling ANGER and EnVY, because they bad feelings and actually are sins, actually are in Top Seven List of sins. Now Joe feeling nothing for Paul or puppets.
It dark at travel town

## August 20

There a movie Joe must see!
Joe is talking a little about self while sell tacos to YOUTUBERs. Out loud. And on purpose! Not writing in he diary He talk out loud about some of he life and feelins. Youtubers listen and one tell Joe all about The Movie!
Movie about Dickhead, excuse me Dickhead MESSIAH (sorry and NOT) From what Joe hear it this VHS movie made just for Joe. Apparently it long movie abou Jesus ggetting whipped (yes!) an d kicked (yes!) and a stern talking to and carrying heavy wood and YEs yes yes!

Joe is down for that. Hope it 12 hour long! **"PASSION OF CHRIST!"**

THERE IS A GOD!

## Friday

More good news!

pretty girl (Goth) from group talking to Joe. She want do something with Joe! This exciting for Joe. A date? IF so it a first for Joe. From what Joe Understand of dates, it all end well (winking)

She taking Joe to something called Wren Fair. Sound kinky – says there is a costume involved.

Expect a SEXY report tomorrow night dear reader ---- unlees Joe is too spent! (winking)

## Saturday

OH SHIT!☹

## August 28

I'm SERIOUS! It all dress up. "Squire this and me lady here and there".

Excuse Joe. He must trhow up.

Again!

## Is Septumber

Joe watch **THE PAAASIONS OF CRFHIST!**

All I can say is it was over too soosn! The 12 hours just shot by! WOW! I've never felt so so good!

He is hit. With fist. With Sword. Sword handle. He push down stairs. He whip. The whip has hooks: when pull out it RIIIIIP

Come off Jesus skin! He scream.

Joe never imagine all the bad things that can be done to Sucker JC. Jesus being beat up all day long for this fine movie.

I'm beat from all the laughing and whacking of (8 times)!

## Septumber 2

I am HIGH! And not on life, Pastor Jim! I'm high on a misxture of couffing syrup and a whipping cream CAN-- if you messs with the cap on CAN just right you can get only AIR INSIDE and breath it in your mouth and WOW!

I learned sly combination from my new frriend Lucas. I kicked Lucas in the head tonight! (not to worry all turn out OK-A)

Here what happen:

I was happy from watching "PAssion OF CHRIST" again (third time) so happy and gleeful that Joe have to go outside. Joe want to sing out - he so happy

Lucas was sitting on Hollywood Bouldvard, just sitting on the sidwalk near he tent and I thought, "Man, it would be fun to kick him, just like in the movie" - there lots of kicking Jesus and whipping him in the movie BUT,

but NO ONE KICKED HIM IN THE HEAD! Well, now it Joe turn! So I just kicked Lucas. In the head!

Lucas is weak and poor.. Jesus always say 'help the weak and poor' so instead Joe is KICKING HIM IN HEAD!

Then Lucas head hurt and Joe feel good and bad at same time: NOT feeling regret and "lesson learned" from Bible Story: NOT that but

WWHATEVER! Lucas and I are now friends. He just left Joe Place after teachin me the new trick with the Couff surup and the Whip Cream! We will hang out again for sur.

I'm HIGH!

## September 9

News alert. Headline: Joe McPuppet to Watch Porno

Here story: Miguel say "better than Porno". Miguel is friend who fix Joe 87 Civic. Also tan (like Tan Guy -the little guy) but he a Mexican Ameriacan. And Joe friend.

He say "Better than Porno, Joe" about something or other, is apparently something people say'

Walk home. If Porno is the best (or Second best?) What is? Joe never never never seen it. He know a few things for saur.

Naked people

There is sex

Sex is bad.

Not sure on 3, these things Joe told by suspect source – parent an d preachers.

## Monday

Deed done! Joe now seen sixth video all time – it a porno!

Joe ranks them here:

6 )"Wagon East" – has great John Candy but where the magic? Magic is missin

5) Unforgiven – all wrong

Porno

Gay sex porno. Homosezulaity is SEX Joe has learned. And it interesting things they do with penis an a butt, you would not believe

2) Harry Crumb. A classic

And PASSION OF CHRIST – still number #1!

Fantastic film is Passion of Christ! SO good! Hurting and Hurting and hurthing! So much hurt! And who getting hurt, you ask? Why Joe favorite is answer. Is Jesus Christ. He get he butt kicked through out movie. Is non stop HURT for He!

Yes Miguel, there is something better than porn!

## September 14

Braveheart sucks. It directd by Mel Gibson who (Tan guy is telling Joe and seling him video) is director of Passion of Christ. So Joe gobble tha right up!

But boooooooring and looooooooong. Everyone wearing very strange make up and have speech impediment. Cannot understand tham! Only good part at the end when they hurt Mel Gibson. Tak a very long time to die and hurt a lot indeed. And he die.

Joe disappointed in Mel Gibson. He have two things going for him:

HE likes to hurt himself **(ONE)**

(two) He likes hurting Jesus Christ even **BETTER**

Braveheart is missing #2 : most important element!

## Septumber 15

AN APPOLOGY TO MR. GIBSON

JOe think and think about last thing he write: about Mel gibson Braveheart sucking! Joe say some very hurtful words

**Joe Apology: Im sorry mr. Gibson, Jo was heady and abrupt because i have a history with that mouther fucker, but that my business alone and I apologize deeply.**

**Mr. Gibson, you clearly hate Jessus more than me!**
**Im jealous! How do you do it?**

## September 19

Allow me to introduce myself. I'm Jack Grey. This is not my real name. Nor it is Jackob Gradus. Nor is it Jeremy Glassner. These are names I have used in the past. I generally do stick to some variation on these initials – J & G. Which is why I find it astounding that my host and current benefactor, Joe McClain, if that is his real name, insists on calling me E.B.

There is a lot to wonder about this man. But I must insist that he is a good man.

For example, I now sit alone in his apartment, which is no Taj Mahal, but it is filled with many items, all of them brand new, that a man without a home would gladly take. He would sell them, this man, and buy drugs or booze or women, whatever was his particular poison.

For all my host knows, I am that man. My clothes are tattered. I am unshaven and dirty. I live among the homeless now. A self-imposed sentence? Perhaps. I have research to do, plans to make, and this lowly state does afford some cover. But I also need to suffer. Or, to make a finer point, I need to make my internal suffering manifest.

And so, this is how I found Joe. Last night he was fighting four men in an alley. These were helpless men, lost men. I found myself drawn to this whirling demon, his complete surrender to anger, to his utter lack of remorse, or was it a lack of worry about recompense?

Intrigued, I allowed myself to become the fifth man who he hurt that evening.

Then we got to talking.

And we ended up back here. No sex. No more need to hurt. To be honest, I would have accepted both from him. For a warm bed? No, for a belief in love.

I don't believe in a real love. But I am amazed that Joe McCain would motor off this morning in his little beat-up car with his little taco cart and just leave a desperate awful man like me here.

But I won't take Joe McClain's stuff. Mostly because I have means he doesn't know about.

But I lie, it's because I'm damned and Joe isn't!

I'll write this here and Joe can rip the page out later, but, even if you didn't read it, it was good knowing you.

EB

## Septumber 20

You meet Joe roommate but you not know how good he can talk!
Believe me - YOU HAVE NVER HEARD TALK LIKE THIS!
HE IS BARRABAS!
HE IS MY NEW FRIEND!

Heres's EB: to tell you story: here he is:

Okay Joe I AM BARRABUS

The crowd asked for a Sacrifice that day. The Romans offered them a choice. One prisoner could go free; the other must die. They could have released Jesus Christ and spared him the pain of the long walk up Calvary hill and his terrible execution there.

But instead they released a horrible misshapen monster. Me.

I am not literally that man. I am me. Jack Grey, Jakob Gerard, Jeremy Glassner. I go by many names. But in this little pit with the ancient VCR, I am known as E.B.

I have read his pages here and I have listened to his ideas, often late at night, our eyes closed, lying on our backs on the roof of this old building. These ideas are not far from mine and they make me long, if only for a moment, to be back among my books and my plans. But, no, these belong buried away, and far from me. For now, at least. They are in a safe place.

He too thinks of the temple. Like mine, his is of this earth, built of dirt and stone, not the fluffy stuff of fairy tales. There is no afterworld in its mortar.

His temple will be built only for one, for him. Maybe this is the difference between Joe and myself. My temple was designed with room for many. Joe has never considered that. It is just for Joe, closed, with high walls to keep out the hated forces of Belief.

Read this Joe. Read it and kick me out of your home. I will not take a thing. Nothing will spare me the horror that you feel entitled to.

Kick me out, or I will once again, tell The Damnation Story, just for you.

## September 24th

E.B. here. Yes, now even I am calling myself that. Why not? No one knows my real name, not even you. So this is E.B.'s final entry in this little tragedy.

I'm moving on. Not because of any lack of kindness on Joe's part, but because I've told him The Damnation Story three times now. And Joe loves it. He laughs and laughs. Tears streaming down his face. And he loves me for telling it. And it's just about the most painful story ever.

So I'll tell it here and pack my bags. And this will be my final gift to Joe, who really doesn't deserve this life, but who does?

He may rip this page from his journal. If so, goodbye.

And now, for Joe. And, as he says on each telling, "WITH FEELING!"

The story of my last sermon.

The setting is a grand church on a cliff. The blue waters of the Pacific Ocean can be seen from the pews, from the altar. Where I stand. Starched white collar and everything else black as death. For this is a funeral.

The funeral of my son.

The hymns have been sung, the prayers repeated, the scripture read. I stand before God's people, "my" people; and I speak my eulogy. It is one word:

"Sinners."

E.B.

Thursday

ALONE! ALONE! ALONE!

again

Friday

Here's the lirics from RIVER DEAP MOUNTAIN HIGH by Tina Turner:

"When you were a young boy did you have a **PUPPPY** that always followd you around I want to be as FAITHFDUL as that Puppy you knoow I always be around!"

And all this time Joe thought this: I thought it was **PUPPET!**

I wasted my life on puppets!

And I wasted my life on JSus!

And I wasted my entire life: which he tell to E.B! Who just left wihtout a Explanation or anything.

No one has ever made me feel so much – he ideas surround Joe and make him warm. I give him name: EB: it just fit him. Now he gone.

That one hurst the most!
BUILD THE TEMPLE!

## September 27

Joe get a surprise! A truck! I go to my spot where Taco Cart is at night, is chained to wall AND trash bin. All gone – cart and chain and lock. Now sitting there in rays of morning sun (poet Joe) is

TRUCK!

All taco truck! All working – stoves and cash register and even gas filled with gas. In the gas tank. Why for?

"JOE" it say in paint on front. "JOE."

On the driver seat is key TWO KEYS: one for truck. One Joe don't know: he look very close at this key: tiny letters say 1234. On other side, say SPRING.

A gift then? Joe think who: Not from Richard J (he still in prison and too far away). Not Pastor Jim or all the loosers. Or Sucker Christ self too lazy and boring and not caring Joe.

No! he only friend: is EB! Must be

## September 28

Test drive.
Look out, Joe! What up ahead? Is that car with John 3:16 bumper sticker? Honk honk! They better look out - here come Joe!

## OCTOBER

This thing Joe to describe: a strange feeling for Joe. He never think this happen again but
He
GOT A TEAM!!!

For truck! "Big job and Joe can't do alone". Ha! The hero talking in movie about Joe Team, like Ocean 12 which Joe see (and own)

The Truck Movie

HERO: "This Big Job! And Joe can't do alone!"

Strong music loud and many pictures appear all over LA Sin City: looking at YouTUBE and Hollwyood Sign and Travel Town and old man house -

Other voice saying: OTHER VOICE: "Here they is. The best."

See Miguel! He **working** on truck engine – Thumb up!

**Goth Guy!** He doing register money - looking sad but doing very good job!

Homeless Willy: he a cook! And do a little salute that look like this: hand in front of face, two fingers out – rest are curled up in palm – he move it from face AWAY from face and (getting this) a little wink as do. Classic!

ENGINE SOUND! And the Team go. Feed the world.

## October 3

Here more about Team. **Not like** puppet team. Joe had team, assistants help with puppets. You see, Joe writes a big show many times and can't make all puppets move and make all puppets talk.

Picture this: Big show at SteadyFaith Church. Joe tell you before of this place, this big deal, big church lots people.

All Joe puppet team crouch behind the curtain – hands up above head – holding puppets. Making move and saying Joe words from script.

On they faces? A smile? Are proud? Are happy? No. Very serious ALL. Even Joe.

NOT on TRUCK! All laughing. Make fun and make food and laugh with team and laugh with people feed.

Is different.

## October 20

Moiney rolling in. Must get back to work on Temple. No more mess around.

MUST work on TEMPLE!

## October 29

THE temple is on hold

JOE IS A SCREENEWRITER!

Taco Customer is telling Joe that movie Passion of Christ is big hit, big money He show Joe on phone: 500 million!

Where the SEQUEL??! THE PASSION 2! ???!

Not to fear! Joe has just the idea: he working it out in head as talk.

## November

New spot for truck. Parking lot near mall – what trip! Joe sneaking off: see Avenger movie (he call it Resarch!) (ha)

It dull. Plus too many characters. Focus, filmmkaers, focus.

Here the equation for you dummies:

One guy
Who get hurt a lot.
Suffer.
He name is JC.

Equals = make a billion dollars.

Lesson learned? Jo e doubt it.

## Wednesday

MOVE OVER HOLLYWOOD!

HERE'S **PASSION +2: REVENGE!**

When you are in the zone, well Joe is in that zone! Notthing stop him : not even chatter chatter of Bozo in GROUP. Joe try to keep mind turn off when Bozo Speaking but then dumb Bozo say:

"blah blah meds blah blah personal integrity blah blah best film ever

(JOE ears perk up)

He continue: "blah blah best film is LORD RINGS: RETURN OF KING."

WHITE LIGHT! The whole thing FLASH in a second in Joe mind and JOe sees it: the movie. The sequel!!! To The Passion of Chrst!!

To remind:

**PASSION 1**: Christfuck hurt alot and dies so terrificially! Well done to Mel Gibson! Hats are off for Mel! Best movie ever! A date flick and a wondereful way to spend a lonely night alone (wink wink)!

End with Jesus dying and fleeing to Heaven. We leave him up there hiding out.

AND NOW!

Joe new inspiration:

**PASSSION #2: THE RETURN OF JESUS TO EARTH**:

For brevity sake, I give you only the trailer: Goes like this:

**DEEP Voic e**
(Maybe John Candy deep AND TOUGH like Johnny C.)
**DEEP VOICE** say:

"After the Rapture. (pause) After a many years of tribulation (a pause) The People of Planet Earth have been waiting (pausing) waiting for A Hero!"

CLOSE UP on the special boy: JESUS looking all pretty

DEEP VOICE AGAIN: "waiting for Jesus Christ."

CLOSE UP ON JESUS FACE NOW: His face is all round and big OVAL MOUTH going "OH SHIT!" Because he scared of:

**ME**: "WAITING TO KICK HIS ASS!"

You see Jesus forget about me waiting for him. Who you going to call when Rapture happen? Not calling Ghostbuster (a laugh riot, BTW) not calling the army not calling president. NO, you going to call JOE MC FUCKING PUPPET!!! of course

Back to trailer:

All the people of earth surround Jesus! And me and Mel Gibson are there. That Jesus is in trouble now

**The Trailer ENDS** like this: JOE MCPUPPET (me) pulling out a rocket grenade launcher from my pocket and saying (two shot) to Mel: "You want to light this candle?"

MEL: "You hate him more than me old freind! Fuck him up!"

Me: Okay!

Last shot of TRAILER: **KA FUCKING BOOM!**

Now let you mind work a little and you can imagine how cool Mel and me can make that look -- like him swallowing the damn grenade in his mouth, "Oh shit GULP" down the tube to tummy A high five on my part from all of my friends in this world, Mel included, all laughing: We counting down together: "3, 2, 1!"

**KABOOOOOOOM!** The splatter will annoy you and at the same time give you the biggest stiffy you ever had unless you are a girl and then you get wet.

Wow! This movie is going to Rule. Gim me a call, Hollywood.

Or don't you like money? **$**

## Friday

Joe spent. Too tired from working. Too tired even Passion O Christ; whack in bathroom: Too tiered.

Instead: in bed: listening and watching my own movie: you know the one! PASSION 2!

(wink wink) hope your nights are as sweet as Joe'S!

## Noever 9

SOOOO SICK!

"1234." Joe just lying there. " Spring." Joe holding key EB leave → Joe turning over and back and saying over and over 1234 and Spring. What mean?!

Dear Brain, please stop hurting! I have a temple to build and a movie to make!

MEL?!!

## November 11

Do the birds that sing outside my windo have souls?

Does the Red Dog that licks my hand in the morning and makes Joe happy for a moment on his way to all his evil shit? HAVE A SOUL?

Wha about that little grey cat who sits under the wheel of a car -- does that sweet fragile little thing have a soul? He breaks Joe's heart

How about All the Gerbils Joe "loaned" to little special childerrn in Church Schoo? Joe say to kids, "you go now and bond with little Gerbil.". Next week, kids are crying "oh Joe oh Joe, Gerbil die, gerbil is dead." What Joe do then? Well, Joe counsel these little kids and say "There is the story of the RAINBOW BRIDBE, a placer where the animals wait for you and play all day and all night, happy and together. They waiting. Then one day waiting is over: then they wag their tail real hard or meow real loud or go "Chuck chuck" (that that sound gerbil make) and say, "My master is here to get me" and all lick and cuddle you and you cross the Rainbow bridge together to the most wonderful place of all, Hevean, and you are together forever."

Question for JOe: Is this even true, JOe ? what's the answer:

JOE: I DON'T know.

Joe has been to the place where All Answers are kept and none were forthcoming.

JBecause Jesus is a real JERK who cares so littttle that he'd rather let us all WONDER and NEVER TELL US!

Damn. Joe feel ripped off big time.

## (10 days later)

Joe back. Tough time last week. Goth Guy now has new name. Super Goth! Joe pass out at work. Joe not hear or see this: but all around everybody like: what do? "What do?!"

Up step Super Goth! (Joe see in mind like he rip Morrisey shirt in half to show SG symbol on chest.) (A laugh)

Off fly SG with JMCP to find this house. 2 friends of Goth live there: they doctors. Sooooooooo kind and treat Joe.

Is week later – all resting and recuperationg at Todd an David place. They sure swinging bachelors in they pad. All friends over to party party party No chicks to slowing them down. Easy life. They even same size and share clothes – Thrifty! Like same food and same mov ie.

Joe going back home now but he new friends say "Always room for Joe." Joe say a little joke: "not until you marry and wives kick Joe out." That get bigger laugh than Joe think and happy :"Always room for Joe." I like that!

## Noeber 22

Miguel is whiz and find new place for truck so now at NEW PLACE. There is a TV show now they making it here and Miguel cousin Jorge he working on it, he build sets. This big job because the place they shoot TV show is just a warehouse. But now inside is like a whole city – a city and they making new parts everyday – a different room, a big room or little, or now even the top of a tower in Paris or street in New York City All inside this warehouse.

## November 25

Joe = caterer. At they lunch break, all Movie People come out for Joe food. They even bring own tables and chairs – that is someone job. Not Joe.

Joe observe:

Crew is all working and making TV
They is sorted up in categories - each with name: Grip is one. Dolly is another. Also Camera and Electric. Like nicknames but also describe how work.
"Creatives" is never seen, is invisible or eat somewhere else.
Favorite: Actors. They can be male or girl (boy or girl). They job is to be someone else. "That Joe Job!" he say and HA HA many laughs all around with actors. Joe like them and they like Joe.

## November 27

More good times with actors. Sometimes they "rehearse" (is rememberin) and go like this:
ACTOR: "The image is not clear. Can you enhance that?"
Other actor say: "Coming right up, boss. There!"
ACTOR: "Oh my god!"
All is pretty people. Pretty girl and pretty boys. Very clean.
Biggest Actor is Star. Star is nam James Caan. All call him Jimmy Jimmy not clean or pretty he tough. This last is just Joe hearing this fact: he has not meet Jimmy Can. Not yet.

## Friday

Today working hard and selling tacos. All actors sit around eat and talking.
They talking about Christmas (is that time) and one say
"Joe where you Christmas tree?>"
Miguel say: "Joe not a fan."
So pretty girl with blond hair that glow say: "what gives, Joe?"
Joe say: "When I look at a tree, I don't want to have to think about Jesus."
Someone: "You no believe in Christ?"
Then Willy (Homeless Willy) he grab a chair and sit down, putting hands behind he head. "Here he go folks. Here he go."
Joe say: "I have much to say on that subject." And then Joe got a speech and

he give to actors, saying outloud. Go like this: from Joe memory:
**"SACRIFICE"** is word everyone use to describing Jesus: he **"SACRIFICE"**

Really? Let's us look at it:

Who is Jesus: Let's look at it: a Heavenly being, unlike you and me, born to heaven, He's GOD' S SON!

Born in Heaven? SUre. Born to the most perfect Father of all time? Sure.

Privileged! That the word. Sometimes people call him " Oh, the Son of Man.' No, he "Son of GOD!" He Daddy is richest ever, most powerful ever. Our Jesus is Rich Kid! He privileged and down right spoiled.

So - does Rich Kid Jesus do what other rich Kids do with spare time? Does he join Peace Corpse or go protest bad things? NO. He content at home. He call it Heaven:

Then Dad say: "Son, go to Earth. It part of my plan."

Jesus sleepy but say "okay dad.'

Jesus goes and it is a PARTY and everyone following a Eastern Star to meet him and giving him presents and old men in temples sayin he is the Best and the Smartest THEN people just love him and follow him around. He can do anything! Get away with! He trash the temple and he kick stuff around (a lot to like here) He do magic with water and bread and fish - "waa laa, lots more of that now folks!"

Then he die. But not for long. He back and what he do now? Kick ass on bad guys? UNDEAD JESUS VS. ROMANS? Joe pay to see that.

Nope!
He say
Bye bye and WHOOSH upstairs.

Now he back in Heaven. DAD (God) is saying: "Nice Job."

And Jesus thinking, "I did a wonderful thing for Mankind." And he sink sink sink into he couch. NEVER TO GET BACK UP!

How you call that "sacrifice."? Why we celebrate that?
NO! Joe will not

The end.

## Monday

This day all about Jimmy Caan come out of he trailer and Joe give another speech. Went well, I guess.
Here what happen:
Jimmy coming outside. mUch excitement. He older than Actors, he Star and is tough. He have a special power: like you can't not look at him – he like a magnet. Is his coolness, Joe think.
Actor saying: "Jimmy Meet Joe. Joe has lots to say"
Jimmy: is true?
Joe: I have many thoughts.
"Lay one on me", say Jimmy in he way cool way
So Joe tell one. Like said before I think went well. After, Jimmy shake Joe hand and say "Get load of this kid!"
So that fun.

## Wednesdy

Joe see himself on Youtube. It weird feeling.

## December 2

Joe at work and all saying: We see you on Youtube. We see you on Youtube → Very strange feeling. Can't explain

Joe McPuppet Preaches!

387,019 views - Premiered November 30, 2021

155 4 SHARE SAVE

## December 3

Okay now real weird. Joe not even working. He have day off: at Tan Guy store: Joe looking in video box (the box where the videos are) and people saying: "See you on Youtube." He getting a burrito at shop - never a person say "hi Joe" in there but today: "We seeing you on YoutubE!" What did Joe say? Joe want to know:

Well, he can know Exactly He "trascibing' now - is on Youtube of Course!
Here go: Joe speech to Jimmy all on Youtube:

## JOE SPEECH

Joe: "I have many thoughts."

There is Jimmy Can saying: "Lay it on me."

Joe has a theory: Joe examing all the Known evidence and he Personal Experience and History of Mankind and now he know The TRUTH! A previous theory IMPROVED!

THEORY BEGINS: Imagine some guy you know: some rich kid! He's growing up in a real nice place with a lot of comfy stuff and a very powerful dad. This kid: what he life like?

Well, Dad want him to take over the factory or whatever (this a metaphor for you Jimmy)

But this kid he **has DREAMS and** he has aspirations! He wants to stick it to the old man and HEad out on his own!

Go new places! MAKE his own name!

Kid leaves home: see ya pops!

Dad: "Good Luck, this will end badly I know"

Imagine this now: This kid, this privileged kid, the MOST privileged kid in all of history with the powerful father, the MOST powerful Father of all time. The kid name is JESUS! And Jesus is gonna REBEL and BIG time!

He say: "I am out of Here" (out of heaven) and he is off to Dad's old kicking grounds where Dad made everything, I mean EVERYTHING - is Earth!

Son saying: "Check me out!" and he get born in a little barn, just like that!

Then he grow and get a job cutting wood up and putting together as something new: Chairs or a table. Here funny about this part: this dummy not even know he actually trying to be just like Daddy: making something new (like a World, a Earth) What a Dummy he don't even see it!

All this is not enough for Jesus. He want to be famous: so he doing miracles, "waa laa, you no longer sick, waa laa, you no longer dead! How about that folks!"

It working - people staring to recognize him. First is John the Babtist: Is like: "That dude look like God!" "He is God!"

What a a party! **Dude is a ROCK STAR!**

Got him Bunch of groupies, And he got like a band, 12 dudes follow him around, Jesus making sex with Mary Magdalene, really showing he Dad that he "The Man"

He is TOTALLY going for it now doing unnatural stuff like making more dead people get up and talk and hug him. And piss? And make sex? (with a dead guy?! No thanks you Goth you.) (is joke, Jimmy)

There only one real Cool guy among them: and name is Judas: and he say "Cool it" to Jesus.

Oh boy is that wrong thing say Jesus not want to hear that. He want to hear "Chug it!" or "do the whole pile dude!" He rock star!!!

AND soooo

ONTO JERUSELUM and what do? Kick over shit in Temple (joe admire this) and piss off everyone and make self a big PAIN In Ass to all!

for what reason? THAT is reall question, so let us examine:

**Answer 1) the cool reason:** he really meant it, he meant this: FUCK IT! He meant that his whole trip to earth had a real MESSAGE which was "FUCK IT!" Fuck this place, and fuck how his father set it up, because we ALL DIE and FUCK people who try to make SENDSE of it all and ESPECIALLY fuck them who think they got it ALL FIGURED OUT!

In this case, JESUS would remain Joe hero (despite our history) and be best answer!

**Answer 2) What is? Here a hint:** Ring Ring – is phone ringing in Heaven.

God: Hello, who there, it is late to be calling.

JC: is me Dad.

God: Son, I been so worried.

JC: Daddy they mean to me. Everybody so mean to me. Daddy I want to come home!

God (Dad): You got it son. I fix everything. You have to die first but then you come home, okay?

JC: All good, dad

So, when they tell you about the way Jesus suffer so Nobly is lie. Little pussy had a smile on he face!

All 50 lashes - "Big deal, On my way home to daddy!"

Dragging Cross up hill: "OK-A with JC. Comfy Couch in room is waiting, here I come!"

And on the cross he wink and giggle a little and say "It is finished"

And now JOE IS FINISHED!

On the Youtube is now picture of Jimmy Caan Coming up to Joe and shaking hand and saying "Get a load of this kid!"

## December 4

"VIRAL VIDEO". What is?

# The Prophet of the Taco Truck

by Barry Lange

It's just a normal parking lot. We all park in one of these every day, going to the office, going to the supermarket, or shopping at the mall. The only thing out of the ordinary is the old woman with the pink hair waving a brightly colored sign. It reads, "He knows the truth!"

The taco truck looks normal as well. Men delivering tacos and other delights to hungry workers or shoppers. What's not normal is the size of the crowd. Some come for the food. Some for the show. All have come to hear the "Prophet of the Taco Truck."

He calls himself "Joe McPuppet." What his real name is, or where he comes from, is a mystery.

His physical appearance unfolds slowly on you. At first, one is drawn to the line of stitches that part the side of his head where no hair will grow. But soon, one is drawn to his eyes. Joe's eye are [illegible] describe. Almost translu[illegible] staring, alwa[illegible] mista[illegible]

## December 5

This is not good. Same truck. Same place. Same people - except more! Manny many more!!!

All want Joe, more Joe theories. All phones in air - point at Joe. He hiding. I am crouched in corner of truck, down low Can still see phones - they hovering over him.

I don't like this.

## It a week later

Here is Joe now: is dark and below ground. Concret walls sometimes wet. There one light - it on wall. Is above door

Sort of circle of light. IN circle lives cot and blanket and chair and Joe. Outside circle, room go on and on but all covered. Covered with junk.

Somewhere water dripping. Dripping dripping DRIpping.

Joe sit in chair.

## December 11

The Last day before this was terrible. Joe is arriving at work place. Is a pakring lot near beach. Is Waterfront. Is Venice.

Joe look at Truck: it seems like lunch rush but NO – not that time yet. So many people. Joe climb on top of 87 Civic – can see soo many people AND he can see he Team. They in the truck, not serving food, not making food, just standing there.

Someone yell "IS JOE!"

Maybe Joe up on top of car is bad idea – IS bad idea! That when Joe jump and Joe walk away But people are all around. All around Joe with phones up in air. Go like this:
Someone run up to Joe and raise phone over head and smile. Stop. Look at phone.
Repeat.

Someone start saying "JOE MCPUPPET JOE MCPUPPET" then all saying "JOE MCPUPPET JOE MCPUPPET." Like that. Like a party all laughing, happy

Then someone go grab Joe: someone hug Joe: someone kiss Joe.

Someone stick hand in front Joe. Joe just grab it, Joe shake it – automatic.
Guy: yelling: "He touch me!" He overjoyed saying "Joe touch me!"

Now all hands reaching out to Joe! Joe is touching hands Joe is running People is running. Joe is on the sand. Joe I n the water.

Now Joe here. EB place.

## in December

All around Joe is much stuff. Pile and pile of stuff. Like too much. Like bag and bags full of something TV Guide. Joe try count the TV guides. Give up. A plastic bag full of doll clothes. Why? Joe give up.

Outside - no one know I here: this place. I never leave.

That day: Cab Driver did not think it here. Cab Driver think it not exist, he think Joe maybe crazy anyway - Joe with wet clothes running down street in Vencice, he jumping in car and yelling "1234 Jump!" 1234 Jump!

Cab Driver look at money All Joe money In He hands. Say "Jump street?" and "No such thing as Jump street."

Joe: "Is Spring?"

"Spring Street? DOwntown"? say Cabdriver.

Joe: Sure thing!

Joe don't know He just remember number on Key He believe. He have to believe. When Cab Driver is on Spring St and shake he head "no 1234. There 1232 and 1236 but no 1234." Joe jump out anyway There is no number but there is stairs. Joe follow stairs down and down below ground. He have he Lucky Key Door open.

Here is Joe.

## December 13

Who **WHO** does Joe talk to now?

I hoping that you believe it by now: that Joe use to drop on a knee Every Night from age 3 to age 16 until tumor in brain got too big and then Gabriel kneel for me beside hospital bed: we pray together then.

Who did Joe talk to BACK then: Jesus and God. Who Joe talk to now?

Well 1) Jesus is out! Those prayers head nowhere! Joe will be pour heart out and JC be trying to cue up Dark Side of Moon to Wizar Oz or lighting he farts. So HE OUT!

2) God. God is what Grief Group call a Enabler. JC problem is his problem too. So NO to God.

How about 3: and Joe tries a new religion? Go Hindu or something. Sound too much like Goth and that not going to work out for Joe McPuppet.

No! I am alone.

## DECEMBER 14

JOe was once in a hospital for a very long time so he know a thing or two: Topic is: Suicide

Knowledge is: suicide attempt usually one or two things:

Is release from pain so you go to a Better Place. Where Joe going to go if he die? You saying that Heaven equals Better Place? NO! Joe has been there and no plans to go back!

2 - A CRY for **Help!** If this is true, Who is Joe calling? Sucker Savior?! Ask HIM for help? Where he when Joe was at Gates of Heaven? ANSWER: He out buying a VHS of movie "Beachs" (which suck). And he already own copy. This is his back-up!

Meanwhile, Joe is waiting at Pearly Gates: Joe is all the time humming and waiting – he weighing Handshake vs. Hug and wondering about the beard (did he keep it?) but NO SHOW!!

So I ask you: Does Joe ask for Help there? Does Joe CRY? No.

Suicide is out.

## DEcember?

Dream: is voice saying "40 days in desert."

## DE cember 16?

Some knock at door. Mysterious package outside. Joe throw it on pile.

## DE cember 18?

Joe listen to dripping dripping and looking at all that junk. He looking and then he staring and then he Studying. What find?

A path. Yes, a path through piles. He follow: is tight. What find?

Another room. Is sooooooooo different: everywhere is junk but NOT here: here is tidy and clean.

There are many file cabinets. They full of paper and diagrams and all sort of things you find on paper. Tidy and clean. As joe is looking at them: he is remembering EB:

He remembing: EB say once he have secret. Say he have plans.

Joe remember this: EB at Joe place is always fiddling with something: he technical: he fixing Joe VCR and he TV and work so much better; Even make faster Joe 87 Civic which is gone now

Joe releziing all these things are gone now But EB give him this:

Give him these papers for Joe to figure out. SO Joe is going to do that!

## DEcember 19?

Joe read and read and think and think. What is?
No idea. No idea no idea.

Then Joe have a dream that fix it all:
JOE HAVCE A NICE DREAM FOR A CHANGEE

In dream: Joe is dying and then Dead. Joe finding self Surrounded by other dead people. All are new to being Dead.

VOICE: They are blessed! But You will not see them again! (They disappear, dead people are gone.)
VOICE AGAIN: You alone for Eternity!

Then flame and more flames and each lovelier than the last.

Roll Credits. Speecial thanks to: Old pal Mel, and EB.
And Joe is hopoing to see them both there when WAKE UP!

And he know now what it all is:

IS EB TEMPLE!

## in DE cember

Joe is right. He study papers and yes it is plans for The Temple!

It not JOE TEMPLE: that Joe life work: to build a temple: a place where Joe can stay forever on THIS EARTH, never back to pain of Heaven.

Like Hubert Eaton is the Builder: The Builder have he Temple: is Forest Lawn Cemetery special place. Builder write in his creed for all to read:

"I shalll endeavor to build Forest Lawn as Different. As unlike Other cemetaries as Sunshine is to Darkness. As Eternal life is unlike Death."

He smar man: he saying: "Darkness better than Sun. Death better than eternal Life."

Like the Goths who find graves and such so enticing and they never going to leave them because they don't believe and will just stay there and look sad but be happy inside.

EB Temple involve many big ideas. And it involve destruction.

**This much** I know:

**There are Three (3) PILLARS to EB Temple. And there are three (3) file cabinets**

These three pillars are so named because they alone hold up the entirety of the construct which is society. Destroy one or two and you have mortally injured the beast; destroy all three and the ground will be fertile. Something will grow here. Something wonderful.

The pillars are Government, Church and [illegible]

EB has built a paper machine: that is what all these files and drawings and maps are: they is a mechanism to launch these things that will happen. Destroying the three pillars: When that happens then they will become part of Temple and Temple will be complete.

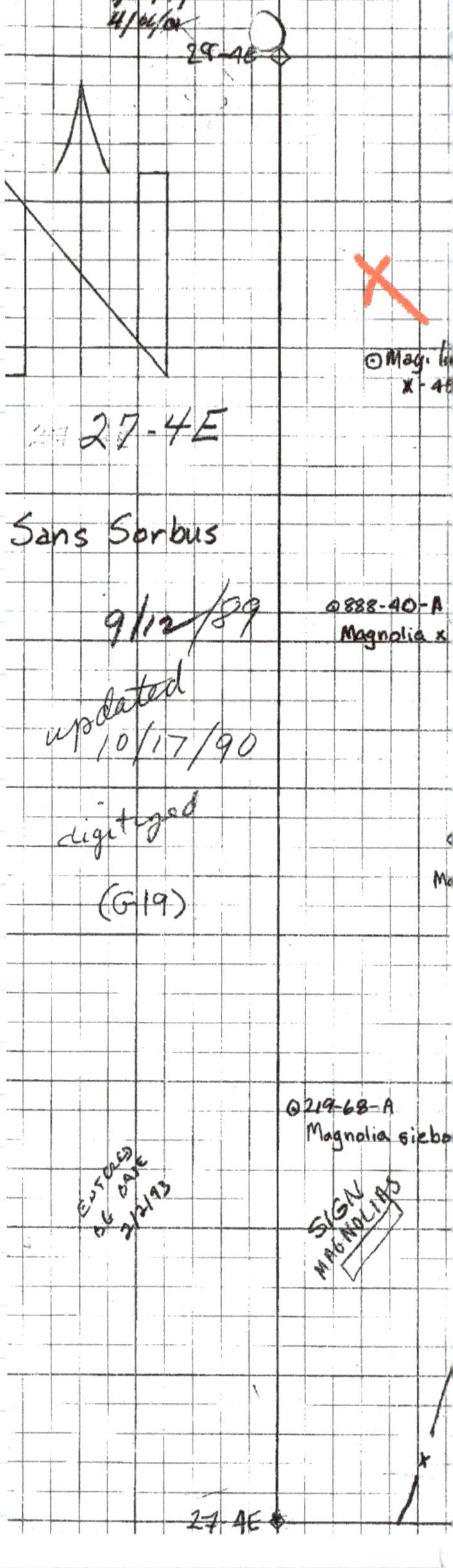


## Dember still, Joe think

Here what keeping Joe up. And joe up all time now seems. At least Joe eat again.

Observeant reader will have noticed → The name of one of the pillars is crossed out: Cannot read the third pillar!

Joe discover (and this releated to that) is all paper is sorted in three file cabinet. Big cabinet have NOTE on: says "Government." Middle one is saying "Church"
Last one: is empty! Nothing in it!

A mystery

Joe move the cabinet and find:
Map!

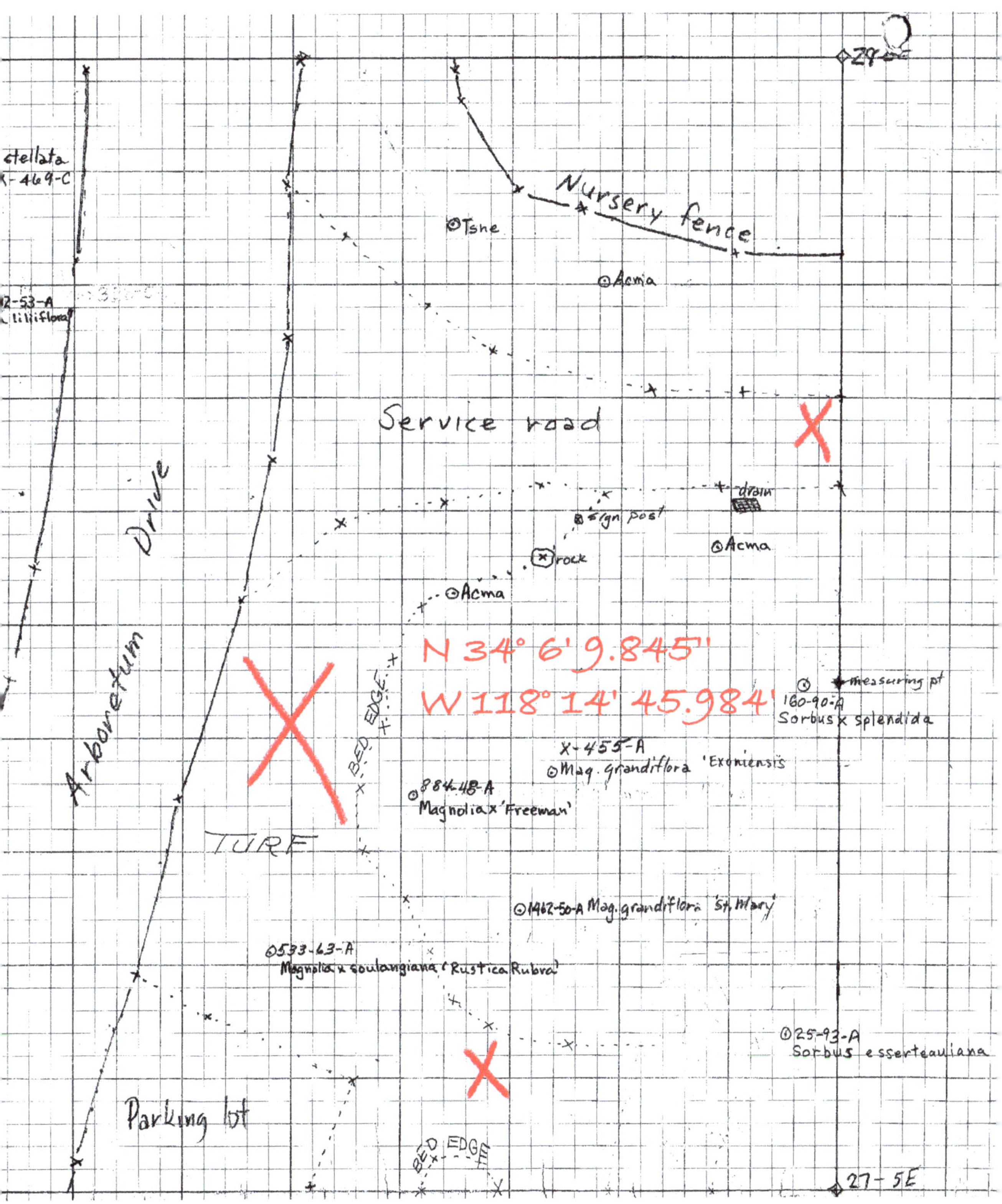

stellata
-469-C
2-53-A
liliiflora
Nursery fence
Tsne
Acma
Service road
drain
sign post
rock
Acma
Acma
Arboretum Drive
N 34° 6' 9.845'
W 118° 14' 45.984'
measuring pt
160-90-A
Sorbus x splendida
X-455-A
Mag. grandiflora 'Exoniensis'
884-48-A
Magnolia x 'Freeman'
BED EDGE
TURF
1462-50-A Mag. grandiflora 'St. Mary'
533-63-A
Magnolia x soulangiana 'Rustica Rubra'
25-93-A
Sorbus esserteauiana
Parking lot
BED EDGE
27-5E

## DEcember 22

Picture this: Joe is in a little space behind the rectory He is holding EB instrument. It GPS and it reading exact number next to red X on map. N 34" 6' 9.845 and so forth. There a small hole in the wall near Joe hand. Joe reach in and what? A small string in there.

Hearing: music and singing choir: is church in session on Sunday morning. "All rise" saying Priest and sound of that: all rising. Sound of prayer from a hundred mouth.

Joe look at string. Joe stare at string. It a fuse.

## DEcember 23

Joe back from 7-11. More sandwich and drink for Joe stash. He also bought a lighter.

## DEcember 24

It midnight and sirens finally stopping.

Joe went to Church again today He have he map and he have he lighter. And he have EB in he mind: EB voice:

EB saying: I am BArbarus, Joe. The crowd that day could have spared the man of Peace but they spare me instead. What you think that mean, Joe?

Joe don't know what Joe think. He know what EB think:

EB thinking: I am the opposite of Peace. I am war. I am destruction. Jesus put on Earth to teach one thing. EB here to do another: which is "Destroy All"

Which is why Joe bought lighter and go back to Chruch because EB making sense here. Joe taught whole life what ALL is:
ALL is not what here: Life on Earth.
ALL is what happen AFTER. Is Heaven abovie! And Joe know and Joe been there, that Heaven is not all cracked up to be!

Joe is tired now He hands are black from ashes and Joe has no water to clean them. Fanta (orange soda) will have to work.

That because Joe burn all the files when come back. All the Chruch files. (What Joe know about Government?) HE pull all out to dumpster in alley behind 1234 Spring many trips and dumpster very full. That why fire so big! Manny manny fire engine!

I could not light that fuse. Was sweet sound of choir? Was familiar wordsd read by minister? Because if Christmas eve? Hell no!

It just occurring to me: Joe thinking this in little hole behind Rectory with fuse and lighter in hand: Joe thinking:

"They are all believing. And saying believing out loud. This place important for them : it is place to say "believe" out loud and with all others there!"

Joe remembering before he Know The Lie. How he look around in Church and see people believing. And Joe thinking: "People need to have something believe."

That making Joe joyous? He discovery?!

No making joe sad

What Joe believe in?

## A NEw DAy for JOe

**Jimmy! Joe believe in Jimmy Cann!**

Response: APPROVED
Approval Code: 819543

Sub Total USD$ 25.23
Tip: 3.78

Total USD$ 29.01

The Glory Guys

Funny Lady

Misery

Thanks for supporting local business!

Brian Song

THANK YOU

Honeymoon Vegas

For the Boys

Slither

## December 27

Joe "sleep on it" as say and yes, Jimmy is IT. One to believe in. Trust. Know Joe is right - that is feeling. Feeling CERTAIN! He feel certain.

It all remind Joe of he Confirmation. Is 2nd Baptism. When Baby Joe get dunked and get wet in church - that is firs Baptism. Confirmation is #2, when 13 year old. Both FULL immersion (church believe in this): means Joe completely under water! Big tub of water up there on altar: in church!

Big day in boy life: lots of preparation. Read bible. Memorize. Pray prepare!

Joe must do same for Jimmy

## is 28th

First up in Operation Jimmy is: ELF. Lots of nonsense in this movie with a toy factory and Santa. It really get cooking when Jimmy there. He is tough dad. Rich is Jimmy: and take no lies: is no make believe in he world. There not Hero name of Santa: the annoying man is not an Elf. Jimmy look like he want to beat ALL up ALL the time!

Was worth a trip back to Tan Guy? Worth wearing hat and sunglasses (this Joe disguise)? Worth almost all Joe Money gone for new VCR and manny Jimmy tapes? A big hell yes!

Getting to know my Jimmy

## DeCEMBER 29

Roller ball! What hell this?!!! Joe has no ide what this world is: what planet they on? Jimmy is TOUGHEST but on ROLLER SKATES?!!! Joe must laugh but head also hurts; boring!

## DEcember 30

Mickey Blue Eyes. Now that a movie! What a perfect role for Jimmy – he a gangster for the mob. Bravo casting Agent: you found perfect fit for Jimmy

Also, Freebie and Bean. Jimmy is Freebie. Is a cop. He name is Freebie because he like free stuff. Very relatable. Who don't?

## Deceber 31

Joe almost ready He learn many wonderful things about a Wonderful Man. He 81. He live in Long Beach California which is very fancy (and not far from Joe!) He like New York City and TV (acting and watching) and many manny films.

Tomorrow is Day: Operation JImyy

Remember the night before Confirmation, Joe? Of course! Very nervous – Joe at dark dark church at night (he have key) and looking at altar and at water there: water so calm: waiting for Joe Body Joe will be back tomorrow on Sunday See, when Baby Joe in the water before: Joe cannot speak then: he mom saying words for him. Words of how Joe now give Self to God.

This time Joe say those words.

Now: right now: it also dark and also night. He outside Jimmy house in Long Beach California.

Big house. Nice lawn. A few statues - m,aybe Lions? Tigers? There the door! House white - Door is Red.

He closes eyes: I can imagine Jimmy in the door: standing with light behind him: he glowing.

Tomorrow: Joe say this: he practice it now: saying this to Jimmy Can:

"Good day Mr. Jimmy Can. Allow me introduce self: Name is Joe McPuppet. You may recall from previous meeting. I have a unique life experience that allow me to know many manny things of import. Let me first Briefly relate this experience. IN short: I died. I die at 16 year old and go to Heaven. I seen it: can promise you it real. It exist, Mr. Can.

However this experience is very disappointing: not to go into deteal: suffice to say "someone" did not show up (hint: he go by name of Son of God). Just blew Joe off.

Upon Return Earth, Joe has seen All in new light and he has had many adventures: some good some bad: and he gather information. And now has examined problem and have solution.

I hear today to announce to you the Solution. The world needs a Messenger.

And you, Jimmy Can, are that Messenger!"

That it. Joe will wing the rest – some suggestions on Message, some ideas on how spread Message. Extemporaneous. Just see where Conversation with Jimmy go.

I know subject well and completely prepared and confident all will go well.

Tomorrow!

## Janudrry 1

It worked. Now I live with Jimmy

Very nice. Nice house. Pool. Kitchen. everyting.

How it happen: Joe scrap original plan pretty much imeddiate. Plan survive as far as walk to door, knock on door. Then: Different. Let say: big Men (body gaurds) are running at Joe. He learn a headlock is arm around neck. "What you got there! Buddy!?" Is bag of Jimmy VHS. He learn "chokehold" mean hard to breath. Seeing lots of Jimmy welcome mat: very close look at mat and someone yelling: "IT okay! It Okay! Police on way!"

Then Jimmy appear. "Let me see this kid." They is raising Joe head which is also hurting.

Joe never for get Jimmy shirt: it the lightest of pink and buttons are silver white like pearls: Joe count 8 buttons and one unbuttoned around Jimmy tan neck.

Jimmy looking at Joe: and Jimmy thinking "Know him? Not Know him?"

This Joe only chance. So I tell Jimmy: not my speech: I say: I think I say:

"Sir, I think the world needs help. Maybe a messenger. Maybe I wrong, not sure. But I know one thing: I know that I need a friend."

On Confirmation Day after Joe emerge from cold cold water, the minster says these words: "the Holy Spirit work within you that having been born through water and The Spirit, you may live as a faithful disciple of Jesus Christ."

Jimmy say: "Let's get a beer."

## Still JANUARRy 1, it is later

Jimmy introducing people to Joe.

"Here Joe is Ms. Chiang. She cooks like a goddess so if you get hungry you talk to her, she fix you right up.

Here Joe is Maria and daughter Marta. They keep everything clean. Don't get in way or you regret (winking)

Here Joe is Missy She Jimmy girlfriend. Have a mean back stroke. Watchout!

Here Steven, he drive Jimmy manny cars for him.

Here Peter and Marshall. You met them ha ha and Hector who keep all plants alive.

Here is a little house beside pool. You bunk here.

I make you deal, Joe. You promis Jimmy to get mind and body better, you can stay here long as want. Deal?"

Deal, Jimmy!

## Januarry 5

Here's how it work with me and Jimmy: Here an Example:

Picture this: I am at Jimmy house chilling and must heed the need: the Urge to Purge! " Excusse Joe, Jimmy, I will be in the Loo!" Shut door. Drop down pants (ZIPPP!) ("clunk" too because Joe wear a belt – that sound of belt hitting floor). Then "Ahhhhhh! Is good shitting there at Jimmy's

All done. Okay Up trousers go. A snap. A zipp! All done in here, leaving. (forget something Joe?)

Joe did forget something.
Forget to flush: Jimmy saying later: "Joe you leave me a little present?

JOE: "what say JImmY?"

Jimmy: "A little brown present in a bowl? "

JOE: still not getting it: say: "I don't get it."

Jimmy: "A turd. "

Joe slap head and say SORRY SORRY and Jimmy say: no big deal HA HA HA

**"No big Deal HA HA AH"** I love JimmY!

## Janudrry 7

Another great day with Jimmy

We went to store to get shoes. Jimmy is size 10 1/2 and Joe is size 11. Lots of joshing about this, you can imagine.

Have lunch with Stone Cold Steve: is Wrestler: many funny stories: he and Jimmy friends.
In car: Jimmy have big smile: "Like Ice cream, Joe?" Joe sure does. They go Jimmy favorite place. Turn out both like same!!! Chocolate with chocolate sprinkles on! Which is real good ice cream.

Then back to Long Beach for a nap and Jimmy swim and work out Missy and Joe play cards: she teaching him many card games. Fun!

Jimmy have an idea. It getting dark. "let's take out boat then dinner at Cobra Den." So WHOOSH we drive to dock and WHOOSH we in he motorboat and flying over the water to Avalon (is on an island: is Catalina)

We eating at Cobra Den: food is mostly fish so Jimmy telling best to eat: It all so new to Joe! Some jerk say "Hey The Grandfather" to Jimmy Joe get mad but Jimmy laughing.

On way back, Joe is asking: "what mean?"

Jimmy: "From the movie."

Joe: say: "what?"

Jimmy: "watch the movie, dummy!" and hit me on head real soft and nice. So Joe going to find that movie about a Grand dad and watch Jimmy being in it.

Sleep well that night for sure!

## First day of movie 15 Januarry

Jimmy starting a new movie: going to be very busy: so will Joe. Joe has JOB:

How works:
Jimmy schedule:
He up very early
Car to set (where movie is)
In a room with many clothes for Jimmy
In a chair with make up for Jimmy for movie acting
"Jimmy on set, please"
Jimmy acting. Example: he saying: "Listen punk! I only tell you once!"

"CUT!" They yelling. And Many manny people telling JImmey he so good, which he is.

Repeat.

Where Joe during all this? Joe right there with Jimmy

What joe doing?

Just being there with Jimmy

Joe ask: what my job title. Jimmy say: Title is "pal".

## JAnuary 14

Whoa. Flash from past. Check it out:

Jimmy walking across set, getting a tour of new set from Asisstant Director. Is a big room in Vegas. A casino. Lots of people around: they called extras. Dressed up look like gamblers and people having fun.

Is called "walk-through" so Jimmy is learning where he will walk to and when he will say he line.

Where Joe? Where you think? Right there with Jimmy

About extras: They all looking like party people: until Joe see ONE. NO! Could not be? But is!

Is Paul Hilton. Paul Hilton the Christian Puppeteer! Joe no see since SteadyFaith performance. He sure wowing them there! What doing here?

"What doing here?"

Paul surprise but sort of hug Joe, sort of Careful Hug, holding Joe far from him. Saying: "Lord moves in myserty ways, old friend Joe. I am spreading Word to Hollywood."

Joe getting angry "Word?" he say "Word of who?! Who saying these words you spread?!"

Paul surprisesd agin: Is Jesus.

Joe begin to open mouth but suddenly Joe not standing there no more. He ten feet away Was Jimmy He move Joe with just a little effort: he so strong: and he talking real low to Joe:

"Jimmy hear all. That boy has a job. He thinks that is his job so it is his job. What your job?"

Joe: "Just be with Jimmy"

Jimmy is smiling and say "isn't that better job?"

Joe nodding and saying no more. Because of course Jimmy right. There is no better job then that.

I wave good by to Paul and Paul do that thing he always do after puppet plays:

he raise hands above head like he praying, then dip down below he waist.

Stupid move. That Paul

## JaNuary 15

Joe now has a friend. A great friend. So now is time for Joe to consider difference between a friend and Jesus.

A friend is not the "Son" of anything: except his own father who he not consider a king and certainly not a GOD!
Friend is kind to Joe.
Friend does not BLOW OFF. No matter where he is, Friend is NOT blowing off Joe – weither is a nice place like Cobra Den or a GREAT place like: say: Heaven! You dick!
4 is: Friend is not overly fond of graveyards
#5: Friend will die someday (**shared interest**)

6)Friend (if Male) is cool and not wearing any Robes! And has other friends than just old friends from old days in Jeruseleum. He have a friend like Joe.

AND: (7) that Friend is introducing Joe to Chicks like Missy and one girl at Cobra Den: and NOT saying "Hello, this is Joe who loves God like you do."

Friend is who? Friend is JIMMY!
Love ya, Sport. Long Beach Forever!

These Joe's thoughts on Friendship and he add here that sometimes crying is okay

Janudrry 19

Steven taking Joe a drive in Jimmy Mazaratti. Joe visit Team at Team Taco Truck. All good. Happy see Joe.

Miguel say: "People stop coming looking for Joe, just one guy coming" One guy asking lots of questions like a reporter or police but Miguel not think he either: describe: sound lot like E.B.

Strange.

Miguel also give him $$$ so Joe go back old place. Is Hollywood and Vine. Pay and get old stuff: Steven insist on carrying.

Corcoran State Prison
4001 King Avenue, Corcoran, CA 93212

Prisoner name: Richard Joel Wicker.
Location: Infirmary.
Primary doctor: Peter Preston MD.

Hey Joe! Because of the attack, I am getting out. I look like you now ha ha! I have seen shit on the Other Side like you wouldn't believe except you have been there. I wrote this.

Spiritual Warfare

Cast: Richard Puppet (a battle-scared, handsome man)
Jesus Puppet (solemn. Trusting/has beard)

The scene is Jesus and Richard sitting in front of campfire. Both are roasting hotdogs on long wooden sticks.

Richard: It's really great to finally meet you face to face.

Jesus: This is a nice fire.

Richard: I've had a lot of experience starting fires.

Jesus: That's what I came to talk to you about.

Richard: You don't have to thank me. I accept my mandate to fight Satan and his minions. The modern church is weak. The faith needs warriors like me.

Jesus: I'm not here to thank you. I am here to tell you to stop using violence in my name against those you consider evil.

Richard: Look! The tip of this stick is glowing with heat! Perfect for piercing the heart of a demon!

Richard sticks the stick into Jesus side. A red glow comes from inside the "Jesus" puppet, who screams.

Richard: I make no contract with the devil or the devil's handmaidens! I will continue to rid the world of evil. As long as there is corporeal evil milling around on this planet, the fearless shall make it their destiny to vanquish it!

Jesus: (in demonic voice) Argggh! You may have outwitted me this time, but next time I will bring reinforcements the likes you have never seen! The damned shall rise and tear your flesh from your bones!!!

Richard: Bring it on!

The end.

Huh. Look like Richard J writing puppet plays now

## January 27

POOLSIDE with JIMMY!

Jimmy: "Joey I got a question for you."

Joe: "What that Jimmy?" I say

Jimmy: "Okay Joey let me put it to you straight." Jimmy say this and point at the two little kids in pool. He says: "Church or no Church for them?"

Joe: How much love them?

Jimmy: "They my grandkids. I love them more than live!"

Joe sigh and sip on cool drink and say "Got a moment."

And says Jimmy: "All the time in the world".

Joe tell Jimmy ALL about it. All. Well, we talk and talk and it get night and we still talking with many drinks and finally Joe say: "That all I have to say on the subject."

Jimmy laugh: not what Joe expecting: say: "you one of kind, Joe. That why I like you." Then Serious Jimmy: say: "Tomorrow I show you something."

## JANUARY 28

A big surprise today: Where is Jimmy taking Joe? To a cemetery

Now o course, Joe have mix feelings about cemetery Mainly because of experience with Goths.

But Jimmy have unique perspective: It all turn out to be sort of a presentation: go like this:

Jimmy show Joe a headstone: is his headstone: say "James Caan, March 26, 1940 – " Then Jimmy tell Joe: "Joe, James is my real name." This is big secret and Joe realize now this is Jimmy way of telling Joe that what follows is very important: is:

"Joe, when I took you into my home, I said you could stay as long as you like. This is still true. And I want to you stay for a long time."

He point at headstone: "We all going to die someday I sure don't want to die and maybe you don't want to die even more than me, because of what you've been through."

(He mean Joe being blown off by Big JC)

"I have a good doctor. Let me take you to see him. We can go right now"

What is Joe to do? He go. After all, Jimmy is the Grandfather.

# Patient Treatment Form

Patient Name: Joe McClain Date of Birth: 6/15/2005

**Height:** 6' 2'' **Weight:** 180 lbs. Phone No.: (702) 381-2456

Address:

Reason for Admittance: Cranial Injury

**Appointment Reminder:** Patient will need MRI, scheduled for next Tuesday, 8:00 A.M. IMMEDIATELY

Date Discharged: Physician Approved? ❑ Yes ❑ No

Reason for Discharge: ❑ Patient Deceased ❑ Patient Transferred ❑ Patient Terminated w/o Approval

Diagnosis at Discharge:

Lorens
Signature

02/01/2022
Date

# FRiday

So Joe has new job. Is doozy

Maybe Jimmy trying to keep Joe mind off things: off doctor test: but he sitting down with Joe at breakfast nook and asking for FAVOR.

"O course, Jimmy" say Joe before even swallowing cereal or knowing what is. IS Puppet Play! For Jimmy grandchildren the twins. Is for they birthday party

This hard. Real hard. Joe puppetry and mastery of that art is all out of past: which is church: which is praising: which is Jesus.

Real hard. But. Is Jimmy

I think and thinking: how to do he old puppet plays he wrote but Without all Jesuspraising?

Maybe use his script "It's Adam and Eve, not Adam and Steve" but take out preachy part at end?

Maybe "Model Christian" and keep she a model but lose the Christian part?

Maybe "Heaven Needs Firemen" but when firemen die they don't go to heaven: maybe other Speical place: maybe Disneyland?

Oh boy Joe creative juice is flowing! You crafty fella, Mr. Jimmy Can!

## the 21st

Art store on Beverly Boolevar: Steven dropping off. Steve have errands: Joe saying: take time!

See, Joe don't have old puppets. Mr. Morals, Pastor Bowser, the Candlestick Kids: they all back home.

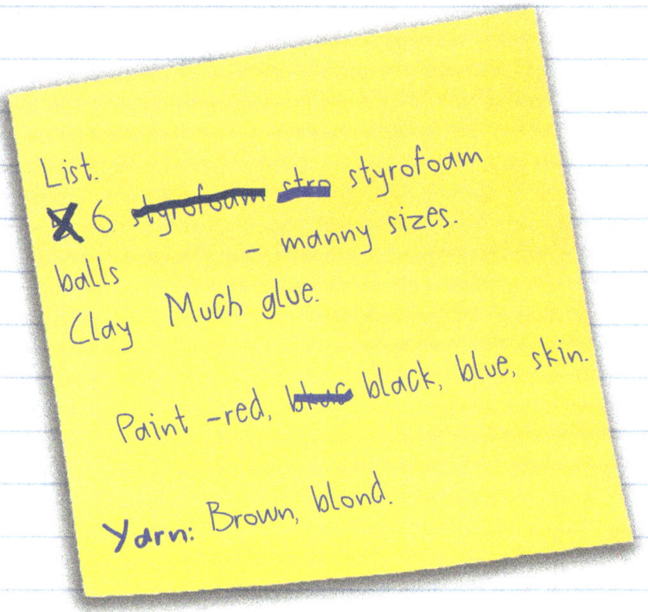


Sometimes Joe writing even hard for Joe read. Ha! So at check out, here is Old Joe staring at list and reading it over and over (he double checking) maybe mumbling: maybe outloud.

Girl there say: "What are you making?"

Joe say: "Puppets" before look up: then do:

Girl is soooooo pretty Dark hair and dark eyes. Very smooth white skin. Is Beautiful. And what she say? What she say to Joe?

"I have some puppets under my bed."

## FerBruay 22th

This weird: Joe building puppet set in Jimmy back yard and Missy come out: say: "someone name Mama Mclain called for you. She wants to visit you. She says EB gave her the number."

E.B.?! IS talking to Joe Mom now! Is weird!

## BIRTHday is this DaY

Big Day! Birthday party for the twins!

This weird day and get weirder and weirder with unseen ending. Buckle up, folks!

Let Joe set scene: setting is Jimmy pool. Lots of Kids running here and there. All dressed like Detectives: is Detective Theme: theme of party All 5 year olds dressed like:

Manny have badges and they saying: "jus the fact mom." One is a dog in trenchcoat: he saying: "take a bite of crime!" One jus having trenchcoat (not a dog): "let me get it straight."

Manny manny Sherlock holmes!

Boy Big party! Jimmy with manny friends. All smiling. There Stone

Cold Steve: he smiling too. There is Missy: all the friends there. Much food much fun

The stage in front of pool house: Curtain and everything: behind Curtain is "backstage": is the inside of pool house.

Action begin: Clown on stage making balloon animals. Joe is back stage getting puppets ready

Who walk in? Richard J walk in!

Well, this a surprise. Richard J calling Joe "Brother" and he do looking like Joe now: he have big scar on head too. It come down from head to one eye which is red.

Turn out Richard J see Joe Viral Video: who knew they have youtube in prison? He say: it change he life.

He say: "It blow my mnd. I have lots time think in bed after attack. Change my life!

Then Richard J look around.

Richard J: "What doing Brother Joe?"

Joe: "I am doing puppet play for friend Jimmy grandkids".

Richard J: he clap hands and leap in air a little: say: "perfect timing!"

And he throw stuff out from he plastic bag: is clothes and bible and then he find: is piece of paper and thrust to Joee.

Here is:

"Spiritual Warfare 2: the Education of Michael

THE SCENE IS A RAVAGED FARM. A GIANT WORM GYRATES SLOWLY IN THE BACKGROUND. A LOW MOANING SOUND IS HEARD FROM OFFSTAGE. TWO PUPPETS (MICHAEL AND RICHARD) APPROACH THE WRITHING WORM.

Michael: Well, Richard, this is it, isn't it?

Richard: You'll know, little brother, when it is "it"!

Michael: Your skills as a warrior have grown and your muscles bulge through your worn sack-cloth.

Richard: I am a true warrior of Faith. One gets strong fighting for the only True Cause.

Michael: And what is that?

(Richard picks up a handful of sand and throws it in Michael's puppet eyes.)

Michael: Aaaagh! I cannot see!

(Richard picks up a large stone and holds it over his head)

Richard: You NEVER see, little brother!

Michael: Please, Richard! Think about your actions!

(Richard crushes Michael's soft head with the stone)

Richard: Thought and Faith are a mysterious couple. To know Thought is to question Faith - to question Thought is to know Faith.

Michael: ooooooh....aaaarghhh...why? Why do you not believe in my faith?

Richard: I thought I did. That is why the answer was so clear to me. Die, little brother.

The worm screams!

The end.

"Very interesting play Richard."

Richard talking talking talking: jist is: is this: "Do play now!" and "For kids!"

This is much different play than Joe have in mind. Is old play Joe do many times for he church: a big hit; he rwewrite for occasion. Here is:

Wake Up Meow Cat, It's A Merry Party Afterall

Cast: Meow Cat
Mommy Meow Cat
Mr. Birthday
Party

Setting: is: Party morning in the living room of Meow Cat family.

Mommy Cat: Wake up Meow Cat! Is Party morning!

Meow Cat: Did I sleep too late and miss Mr. Birthday?

Mommy Cat: No, mr. Birthday ate all he cookies. Look.

Meow Cat: Gee. I like birthday party but I can't believe I miss Mr. Birthday ~~a agin!~~

Mr. Birhday: He! He! He! Is me!

Meow Cat: I so happy I dance and dance and dance.

(Meow Cat dance her funny dance with both paws in air)

Meow Cat: (singing) My whiskers are so soft. Pat them and see.

Mommy Cat: I think Mr. Birthday have something to say.

Mr. Birthday: Yes I do, Mama. Cat. Meow Cat, there is something important I must tell you. Birthday parties are wonderful but do you know the real meaning of Party Day?

Meow Cat: No I do not. I sure wish I did.

Mr. Birthday: Well, the real celebration is for the Birthday Twins! ~~It there~~ Today is they birthday. And here come my good friend, Party, to celebrate!

(Party enters. He waves his hands in his long robe and snaps his fingers.)

Party: It Billy and Scott Jr Five birthday! Let celebrate!!!!

(fire confetti cannon. Play party music.)

Meow Cat: My whiskers are so soft. Happy birthday Billy and Scott Jr!

(all dance)

The end

Clown stick head in: say: "you up!"

Richard saying: "do my play! Free they minds!"

Jimmy sticking head in: say: "show time, pal!"

Joe: (me): Listen, Richard J, I do best can.

Then Joe running through Curtain with all puppets!!!

Play start out pretty good. Kids are liking puppets: especially Meow Cat. They liking so much Joe slow it down: he introduce Floppy Dog on a whim: Crowd loving it: manny manny laughs!

Tjhings go off rails when Richard J can be heard: he backstage but it getting louder and louder. Is praying? Loud!

Joe try to work the whole Spirituual Warfare thing into he play: is off the Cuff: best he can do

"Oh look, here come worm!"

"He! He! He! Is me!"

"I am true Warrior of Faith!"

Instead of rock, Ihave Richard puppet pick up Meow Cat who sing a little song: go like:

"one two, buckle my shoes
Three four, Peter and Marshall listen to me!

Five six, ther is a scary guy behind curtain
Seven eight, get him! Get him! Get him!
Meow"

Then: "Sing with me kids!"

Kids sort of staring: confused: but work!

Jimmy two body gaurds rush through curtain and coming out with Richard J in arms.

Is called headlock! Joe remembers!

He yelling at Joe as go: "Why you forsakeing me?! Why brother Joe?!"

Joe have Meow pupp3et on hand so just say first thing occure him: "My whiskers are so soft."

Very silent now All kids staring: Twins staring.: missy staring: Stone Cold staring: is that Paul Hilton shaking head in disappointmen? No, is just waiter.

But Jimmy sure staring! Is speechless. Is first time joe see that.

It all seem go on forever then a kid say: "Elemenary my deer Watson!"

Joe bow He run. HE going to get th e hell out of there. He run and get to Gate: it lead to street: someone is there. IS GIRL! (forget tell you Joe invite her from Art shop)

Girl smile and say "I love it. Want to see my puppets?"

## 15 morning

So listen up, all friends and foes of Joe McPuppet: this date (the date of this entry) is one for history book: the book on history of Joe: THIS book.

Last night, JOE doing folllowing:
inserting of pennis inside of Girl: Leaving there!:
followed by some moving around: much groan from JOE and from GIRL. Some very nice sounds indeed: folllowed by some Squirtin by Joe with accompanying hooting and hollering!

Repeat process 3 times!

## FEbREuary 25

Joe has read very few secular books but read Llliad by Hommer.
Read it? Joe has.

In this book is story of Helen of Troy: she the one with face that launch a thousand ships.

Girl has face like that: Joe not have ships but if did: he launch them pronto!
This all making Joe wonder; how Girl look at Joe face?!
See: Joe have stitches in head but most ugly thing about Joe: is all pain and disappointment of Rejection of Son of God: Joe show that on he face.
Maybe with Girl, he face soften?

## More FEbruarry

Believe it or not, meet the new Joe. He Joe 2.0. He call: Domestic Joe!

Yes, *NEWS FLASH*: old JOE

-is happy!

-is settling down

-is **happy** for it!

So many good times with Girl. We taking walk on River (There one in LA too it turn out!) near Woodman avenue. We counting birds. Next part will seem like little thing to some: but is big deal for Joe: Girl get cold and Joe give her he jacket!

Never thought happen!

She kind and fun and considerate. Girl love Jacket: wear it all day When Joe having jacket back, he find some trash in pocket, lots of cellophane bags with white stuff and a needle that poke Joe. Girl say: "that is trash: I throw away for you."

Never Joe get so much love and consideration like this!

He meet Girl friends: is another big deal for Joe: It a little smoky in the room but good conversation. Much of they world is new to Joe. But fun to listen. Then Joe get worried: wonder: he good host?: he running around getting chips: but all go to bathroom except Joe (together!) and come out very happy! Girl and friend Arpeeta (I think is name) laugh about some dealer of cards (joe think) Everyone have a story about being ripped off by a card deal. Is a hoot!

Good food. Much talk about cats and cops on take. Very enlightening.

## FEbRURAY 28

It Movie Night for Joe and Girl. What watching? FINALLY is "The

Godfather."
The one with Jimmy! See, Joe getting name wrong: is called "Godfather" not "The Grandfather."
This is "Godfather Number 1" with Jimmy Can as Sonny NEVER BETTER is Jimmy in movie. Never believe he so very good. I will tell all to see this little jewel that time forgetting: is excellint.
Only criticism: Jimmy should not die (spoiler). Jimmy should be Godfather: just Joe opinion.
This all making me think: I need check in with Jimmy Maybe he pissed off at Joe for puppet play fiasco. I need call him

## Friday

Here is Joe: out on Ventura Boulevard: where Girl live (and now live Joe: I guess). Wide streets with manny shops. Just walking along is Joe.
La la la: singing a little song, thinking maybe he be a cat.
Joe the cat: got a cute name like Milo or Little Limpy: then he sleep in bed with Girl all day and all night, always curl up with her. Even though small, Cat Joe would have much love to share.
Such are Joe's thoughts when hear:
"I hear you are back in the puppet game!"
What?! IS Paul Hilton: "You going to catch our show?"

Paul is tilting head up and to side: like over and over: up and to side: then Joe get it: he pointing with head: it a marquee that read "Stars of Tomorrow"
Boy Joe sure was gone to he special place in mind because now he seeing all: he in front theater: lots of people hanging out: all young and pretty: actors!: manny smoking: manny have PUPPETS!!

**Paul hand me this:**

STUDIO CITY THEATRE PRESENTS

# *Stars of Tomorrow*

**THE BEST NEW TALENT ALL IN ONE PLACE. DISCOVER THEM YOURSELF FIRST.**

**The Paul and His Praise Performers present "Hands Reaching For The Stars! A showcase of the best talent in acting and puppetry. Doing it all for God!"**

TICKETS $20
AT DOOR.
$15 FROM TALENT

**THURSDAY**
**MAR 3, 2022**

CONTACT US AT (303) 856 9654

Agents and Managers free admission with identification.

Joe see what other actors see: they see Paul talking to Joe: Paul taking a special interest in Joe: all actors thinking: "Who this guy? Who Paul paying so much interest? Important?" So all gather round.

Paul: "Meet my boys, the best puppet troupe in Hollywood USA."

All Chatter: they doing this monologue or this scene: they recent discover God and he key to they future success: they looking for management.

Joe flee. He look over shoulder and see Paul lifting hands up to heaven and Joe run before Paul do that stupid bow!

## MaRCh first

Big news! Girl quitting! She quitting smoking!

This is apparently very hard to do: and Girl saying this: and showing Joe on phone all Testimony of Experts who saying: "harder than quitting Heroin!"

Joe know a secret: Girl doing this for him: for they life together!

So Joe is very happy but confused: never seen Girl smoke.

## MaRCH

Joe Resume so far:

*Was dead 1:51 minute*

*Hate Christ*

Must find a way to supporting Girl. She doing all hard work by quitting and if Joe tell truth? Well

JOE TRUTH: he thinking about future with Girl and relationship and marriage

Here how work:

After The Tree-Sitting and The Spelling Of The "Kissing": (Check an check!)

then IS:
The Coming OF The LOVe
- then The Coming Of The Marriage.

Then is: The coming of little JOE? In baby carriage?

So many things to learn about Love.

## MORE march

Girl is shivering then HOT all over: she get all farsighted and cannot see Joe face even though right in front of her! Hands shaking: she hear weird stuff: weird dreams.

Man, this quiting of smoking is **REALLY HARD!**

Life so delicate

## MaRCh 31

Girl needs to be alone.
Everything Joe doing is wrong: is making Girl anxious. She yell, "I just need to do this alone!" and "I don't want you see me like this!"
"Like this" equals vomiting and no shower for days.
She too weak to go anywhere. Really cannot even leave apartment! So Joe go. He give her kiss and say "see you in a couple of day"
What she say: say for first time: "I love you, Joe."

**15 April** Joe walk all day. He have deep thought:
A story appear before him like a book opening to a chapter:
Story go:
Here is:

JOE is the same guy he is now EXCEPT there was no accident: he was NOT hit by church bus: Joe just crossed the street that day and not get hit by bus and nothing bad happen that day
SO, Joe just grow up like planned: he not get head injury: he not get cat scan: He not get doctors telling him of growth in brain: He not learning he must have emergency surgery
SO, he NOT dying for 1:51 minutes: and he NOT going to Heaven and you know the rest.

SO, here is Other Joe just crossing the street: perhaps he waving at the passing bus: there is no blood on bumper in this world, in this version of Joe LIFE.
IS alternate World!
So, Joe life is going as planned: by he mom, by he preacher by church community by Pastor Hill and he puppet team.
So, Joe is finishing his schooling at church and school: is receiving the letter he waiting for: the one from school in Ohio: the one where they teach good but teach proper: in God name: Joe getting in!

Here is Joe going to college: he getting all A on papers and being champ of Bible Quiz team: he going to be a minister: he going to have his own church: This is all GOING to HAPPEN for JOE!
Maybe he holding hands in chapel with good girl: maybe Joe going on Missionary work in Africa or Asia or other places: maybe Joe praying a good deal: perhaps Joe becoming good at prayer: lead many people in prayer at he church: very good at job.

All this time, Joe not knowing about brain tumor: which is troubling situation: see, Doctors were very clear on the subject: the brain injury was not caused by bus accident: this accident actually a lucky thing: alerting all to Tumor so Doctors can get it out before it kill Joe for good SO, ultimately **This Joe** will die from the tumor.

SO, all this time: clock is ticking for Other Joe: and HE NOT KNOWING: not knowing that he is going to be BLOWN OFF by someone he love and trust: not knowing that the Son of God who he commit whole life to: the King of Kings is going to BLOW HIM OFF at Heaven gate and not **show up**.
I fell sorry for that Joe! I hope he die soon and get the mystery solve. But the whole thing make me cry a bit: because this: Other Joe is also **Joe**.

## thURSday

Joe walking old haunts: is streets of Hollywood: who find? Lucas. He old friend from Hollywood: still homeless: still good old Lucas.

Joe asking: "Where Mickey?"
Lucas: answering: "Is dead."
Joe asking: "Where Shelly?"
Lucas: answering: "Is in jail."

Conversation go like this for a long time.

Joe sleep last night in tent. He hear sound of street: people shouting then silent: sirens: horns honk honking. Like a little melody for Joe.

But what are words? He straining to hear the words to this meloday

Maybe is a story of Joe and Girl. Maybe Joe living with Girl for all future. Maybe Joe be like Other Joe and living like not knowing what come after. Mabye just live here on Earth with Girl. No need so angry No need a Temple then.

When he woke, Joe is resolved.

Resolve is: Go to EB place tomorrow Burn the rest of the plans. Destroy all plans to build temple. He temple is one of destruction. Joe not want destroy world. He planning on sticking around for a while: on earth: with he and Girl.

THUS:
Joe destroy plans.
Make sense

## APRIL 9

It a long long walk to EB underground hidout. from Hollywood to Spring Street: Joe is walking: it all the way downtown. Sometimes streets are wide as river: sometimes narrow Sometimes crack sidewalks: other: no crack. It raining.

Give Joe plenty time think.

Yes. He right he plan to get rid of EB stuff. Papers there and plans to destroy manny places. Where people work or live or go pray

Joe bring he lighter.

IT seem like black bird follow Joe.

There is: the stairs between 1232 and 1236. They look spooky with rain running down.

Inside (thank to lucky key) here EB place: it even looking more lonely then it looking before: when Joe here it seem to Joe. He same light bulb. He old chair. The dripping And NEW: is a folder. Lying there. Joe never see before.

Dripping so loud it hurting Joe head and

there is Richard J there

Joe low Joe lowest ever been. Forget day learn brain tumor. Forget when blown off by lifelong hero

Low

He spend last days locked in 1234. Chain is all round Joe body: to chair: to floor: He naked.

What can Joe move? Only he one arm. It for turning pages. So Joe can read all in folder. All. All people. All talk Joe life.

Joe going to die. Wish he dead now

**Interview #101**: James Hogar Hill, age 46, DOB: 11/17/1976. Youth pastor, Featherville First Baptist Church, Featherville, Idaho.

Interviewee Hill provided counsel and spiritual guidance to subject McClain during years 2005 to 2021. Hill expresses distress at subject McClain's "sudden change" following operation of 2021. "He made a full 180 degree turn in his Faith." Hill suggests that the absence of subject McClain's biological father in his upbringing contributed to his "backsliding."

Subject McClain's father

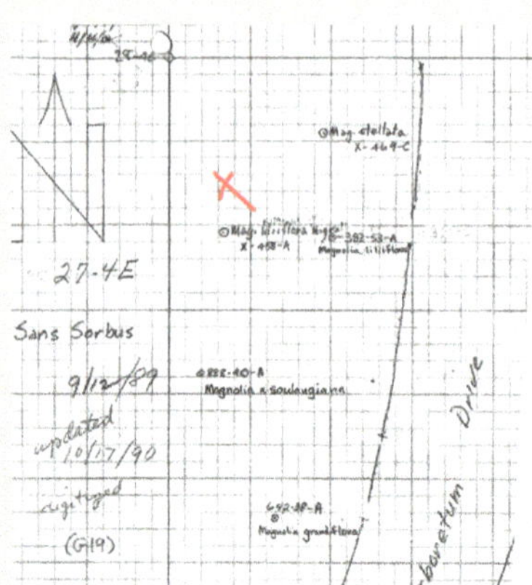


Int
int
Fe
Int
bib
to
No
bib

**Interview #109**: Michael Wicker, 19, classmate at Fe
Baptist Charter. Self-described as "close friend." Intervi
echoes Interviewee Hill (#101) in his description of sub
as devout, studious
Interviewee Wicker shared an event from subject McCla
11. During a performance of a play for the church asser
McClain accidentally knocked a figurine of Christ to the
breaking it. Subject McClain then "cried very very hard,"
Wicker, noting that this behavior was out of character fo
upbeat McClain, who Wicker has known since an early a
event remained in Wicker's memory due to it being unus
because of the close time

**Interview #103:** Gabriel Gilmore, 22, former classmate of subject McClain, friend, church member. Interviewee Gilmore attended to subject McClain before and after his operation of 5/21/2021.

He too notes a massive change
unclear on the specific date of th
Gilmore's recollection of sympto
mood shifts and "not being the
Gilmore shared the same belief
community, which included both
Interviewee Gilmore's emotional
interview from proclamations of
to sadness and empathy for his

**Interview #123:** Donna (would not give last name),
at Featherville First Baptist. Very brief conversation
abrupt termination. Interviewee did express regret f
treatment of Subject McClain, blaming his later beha
decision by church elders to "keep secrets from the

**Interview #108:** Preston W. Johnson, 27, co-worker.
aka Super Goth. Interviewee Johnson was uncooper
However, upon being pressed, Johnson
insisted that McClain wa
man with a messag

**16-#122:** Joanna McClain, 45, mother, aka Mama McPuppet. Note: ok place over several weeks beginning October 8, 2021 and concluding 2022.

s interr
ations w
e releva
r confu
s quotir

First
ker
ain

age
ect
,
d
ally

lso
m

# Cedar Sinai Hospital Beverly Hills

## Patient Treatment Form

Patient Name: *Joe McClain* Date of Birth: *6/15/2005*
Height: *6' 2"* Weight: *180 lbs.* Phone No.: *(702) 381-2456*
Address:
Reason for Admittance: *Cranial Injury*

Appointment Reminder:
*unchecked swelling. All these factors suggest a strong ind...tion*
*of increased deterioration. A prognosis of sudden*

Date Discharged:
Reason for Discharge: ❑ Patient Deceased ❑ ...ated w/o Approval
Diagnosis at Discharge:

...McClain, including a trip to an ... sever... store, McClain's previous residence at the "Seersucker Buil... the post office.

**Interview #114**: Pham Van Ngo, 37, proprietor Hollywo... Electronics and Gifts, 6657 Hollywood Boulevard. Subject visited Ngo's place of business regularly over a 6 month pe... dates unclear. Ngo reports that McClain's interest was ma... ...used on...

...ain's resider

**Interview #126**: Jennifer "Missy" Genari, 27, address unknown, place of work unknow. Declined interview. Ms. Genari was mentioned by Steven Marshall (Interview #113 a recent friend of Subject McClain. Little more is k... ...han her membership in SAG, AF...

...ppears to be ... and tennis instructor.

**Interview #127**: Paul Martin Hilton, 22, actor, puppeteer, founder of "Stars of Tomorrow." Hilton recalled history wit... younger McClain during the time when they both performed "devotions featuring puppets" in local church settings. McClain and Hilton resumed their acq...ship in Los ...eles...

**Interview #132 - #134**: resi...ts of 1511 Vine Street, th... "Seersucker Building." Neighbors of Subject McClain related similar experiences, providing a portrait of a generally quiet, reserved young man with infrequent outbursts of emotion a... loud behavior. Many recalled a period of two to three wee... when several homeless men were seen coming and going ...artment. Identities of these ...n are unkno...

When pressed on this point, intervi... non-responsive. Confronted with statements regarding subject Mc...

***ATTENTION***

further requests for information from this facility would require a court order. Note: interviewee, Joanna McClain (aka McPuppet), very reluctant to discuss her actions during this period of her life. Identity of father remains unknown.

Joseph Hollister McClain, aka McPuppet
DOB: 06/15/2005

## APRIL?

Richard J talking talking talking.

He has new life. He "born agin strong" He have new Belief. He have new Church.
He Belief and he church: equals: The Temple!

Is EB Temple. One of destruction of all and begin new thing in dust of society

Richard J have plan:
Launching EB plan to destroy all. He have maps to manny manny bombs and manny lighters to ignite them.
After destruction: is no leaders: is no God.
Joe become new God: Messiah!

Joe say "fuck it. Joe in."

Because Joe is pretty much dead.
Because he learn
in files
what **ALL the Joes** guess all along
he life built on secrets and lies.
Because Joe see now all HAPPY is illusion: is like Other Joe alternate life: meeting Girl and loving Girl and having friends like Super Goth (Preston?!) and Jimmy: all lies and not real

Because Joe have admit he can never destroy Jesus. He too strong and Joe Kidding self. Is bitter pill.

Do what in staed? Cannot kill God's number 1 favorite creation? How about number 2 - The EARTH!

In summery: Joe agree! Fuck earth and all on!

## still APRIL?

Joe now eating and can walk around room. Richard measure him and go away: return with new clothes: is a costume.

Costume is Golden robes: Golden crown. What for?

Richard J: Is Coronation for Joe!

More on plan: ther is big Easter celebration in desert town: is called Hemet: manny 1000s of people there to see a play on Easter day: what play? Is Crucifixion and Resurrection of Jesus. IT showing all things that happen to Him at end of trip to planet Earth: having goodbye dinner with apostles, in the Garden he talking to God, Judas betrayal, long walk up hill, nails in, Jesus saying "into your hands" THEN 3 days later: he body in cave, all crying then stone roll away revealing - Jesus is Back!

This story very big deal to all Christions.

Richard J: we take it over!

Plan is: interrupt play EB have manny compatriots: Richard J telling Joe this: they who have the will: they take over the play!

Plan part 2: we put on own play Guess who sstar? Joe.

Whatever. This is Joe attitude. Bring it

## APRIL 15

Joe is in back of van. Bump here and bumping there. Going somewhere. Wheere? Joe cannot tell: all windows black. Locked in back of van.

Who driving? Man in hood. He silent whole time Richard J lead Joe up stairs and into van and take off blindfold. He silent now for a hour or more: just driving.

Joe: finally: saying: "That you, EB?"

Off come hood. Joe is right.

EB: "Yes, it is your old friend, EB."

Joe: "How you been?"

EB: "Ups and downs. You know highs and lows. But I am feeling very optimistic now"

Joe: "Because of plan? Destroy society and build Temple?"

EB: "pretty much."

Joe: after long pausing and thinking: "EB, I ask you a question?"

EB: "Go ahead."

Joe: "you have a son who die?"

EB: "Yes, I have told you the story of his funeral."

Joe: "you were a minister?"

EB: making odd sound: just nodding.

Joe: "When son die. Did that change you?"

EB: quiet

Joe: "Joe know all about that."

EB: more sounds: crying?

**No more talk. Bump bump. Going somewhere.**

here Richard J Easterr play

Spirtual Warfare: The Final Blow
The Coronation of Joe Messiah

Scene: Outside of the Tomb. Mary Magdalene and Mary, Mother of James are mourning the death of Jesus.

(This first part is from the BS play as performed by the actors of the Hemet Pageant.)

Mary Magdalene: "Oh, the sorrow I feel is too much to bear."

Mary, Mother of James: "The world has lost its true savior. Let us pray."

The women pray. Suddenly, the rock begins to move.

Mary Magdalene: "Mary, do you see it? The rock moves!"

Mary, Mother of James: "It is a miracle, Mary!"

The rock slides aside and Jesus steps out. He raises his arms.

Jesus: "Grieve no more, for today I am risen!"

(The next part is our play.)

A strong man in warrior garb and carrying the sword of justice enters. He roughly pushes Jesus back into the cave.

Richard: "Back in your hole, false messiah. Your days of tyranny are over."

Several more men enter. They quickly subdue Mary and Mary. (Off-stage, Team 2 is neutralizing the stagehands. Team 3 has already commandeered the light and sound boards.)

Richard: "Listen all! This world as you know it ends today! The Three Pillars will fall. Only the strong of Faith and Will can survive."

Other Warrior: "But we will need a leader, someone who is strong and wise!"

Richard: "Fear not. One will rise!"

Jesus re-enters. (Team 4 has stripped the actor of his costume and Paul has assumed the role of Jesus.)

Jesus: "Please, great warrior. Grant me mercy."

Richard: "You know nothing of Mercy but I will allow you to speak."

Jesus: "I will gladly pass my crown to a stronger warrior. May I please be allowed to witness his arrival?"

Richard: "It is only right. You will place this crown upon his head."

Jesus: "It is fair. I will place this crown on the head of the new King."

The rest of the cast look to the heavens, awaiting the arrival of the New Messiah.

Cast: (various):
"Who is coming?"
"The only one."
"The only one who can save us!"
"He is the only solution. Our only salvation!"
"Without him we are lost"
"Who?"
"Who is it?"
"Who?"

Enter Joe ascending from the Heavens in a Golden robe. (Joe rides a zipline above the heads of the crowd and lands on the stage).

Joe: "Behold, it is I! Joe Messiah! The strong and the wise! I have arrived to build a new world from the debris of the old. As I take the crown, I will affirm my utter dominion over this wretched world. Prepare for Spiritual Warfare!"

(Note to Joe: please feel free to improvise here. Just go with the feeling. Riff, Joe! Have fun and tell the truth of all their lies.)

Joe: (concluding): "I will now take my place upon the throne."

Jesus: "I await your command."

Joe: "Bring the crown."

Jesus steps forward and places the crown on Joe's head.

Richard: "I await the signal, great one."

Joe: "Richard J, go now and light the fuses. The fire will purge all sins. Let it burn!"

# APRIL 16

It night and Joe try to memorize he lines. Boy is a mouthful. He is in tower in town of Hemet: it tower with bells in it: it bell tower. It top of church and overlook the stage and where all will sit tomorrow All empty stage and all empty seats now Tomorrow Joe have best seat in town.

Joe try and try but cannot get into role: Joe Messiah. He no actor but he do know one!

Jimmy: "Hello?"

Joe: "Jimmy it your friend, Joe calling. I don't know if you angry Joe and if so Joe very very sorry Is complicated story but can Joe just ask you one question?"

Jimmy voice is soft and kind. Joe relieved. Jimmy say: "Of course, pal. Fire away"

Joe: "Please tell Joe about acting. How do it?!"

Jimmy think a bit then tell Joe following: "I'll tell you what I tell myself every time I step in front of a camera. Ask yourself two questions. Who is your audience? And what do you want to say about yourself?"

Wow That heavy and a lot to think about. So Joe say: "Thank you, Jimmy I keep you no longer" and he hang up.

So Joe thinking about he own life so far and any time he acting. One thing come to mind: when he is performing puppet plays. Joe close eyes and imagine self at front of SteadyFaith church: the mega church back in Idaho. In the pews are 1,000 people, watching Joe puppets: listening Joe's words.

Joe ask self Jimmy two questions:

Who is he audience? His audience is all good Christians. They all wanting to hear message of hope and Glory of God.

What Joe want to say about self? He want say that "I here to move you." "I here to give you what you want." "Is for Glory of God."

Then Joe stopping and thinking: is he really perform for Glory of God?

Or is it

Glory of JOE!

It hard describe how big this thought be for Joe. Is revelation.

Later: Joe look at zipline. That sure is a long way down to stage.

## SUNDAY

Showtime! Jesus is on the cross and EB just leave tower. He have last words for Joe: is pep talk.

EB: "You and I know more than most the unfair tyranny of the current divinity. God's judgements are random at best, cruel at worst. He takes my young son. He plants a tumor in your head. Jesus is charged with intercession – of showing Mercy to men, forgiveness. As we both know he is slacking off on that job."

He pat Joe arm: then decide to hug: "I leave you to prepare to take your throne."

Joe alone: in robe: he standing by zipline: he waiting he cue.

Below hear Marys crying and stone rolling. There is Jesus. "Grieve no more, for today I am risen!"

Joe head filled with questions: he staring at that Jesus: he doesn't have answers for Joe.

There is Richard J with he sword. There is fighting on stage and in wings.

Richard J: "Listen all! The world as you know it ends today!"

Audience on feet. All shocked.

Other Warrior: "But we will need a leader who is strong and wise."

Soon it Joe turn. He scared and confused. He want to pray but can't
Here is Paul as Jesus. He coming out of cave: he doing he stupid bow move. He voice is deep and loud and he talking directly to crowd.
Jesus Paul: "Great warrior, grant me mercy"
Joe want to pray want to pray
Jesus: "I will place this crown on the head of the New King."
Joe have no Jesus to pray to: only self: so: Joe pray to self: "Joe, please help a frightened and lost soul who is Joe. Guide my hand and help me to make the right decision."

The cast: "Who is coming?" "The only one." "He is coming"
Joe move hand to zipline: what? Hand won't move.
Joe: "In your name I pray Joe, Amen."
Cast: "Without him we are lost." "Who?" "Who is it?" "Who?"
Joe walking away from zipline. Joe sitting down. He crossing legs. Getting comfortable. He not going anywhere.
Cast: "Who?" "Who?"
There a very very long pause. All people on stage is frozen. Just standing there. All looking up.
Somebody: "Who..."
Jesus Paul clearing throat
Richard J: he looking around: he frantic: "I await the signal." He wait then repeat: "I await the signal!"
Jesus: "I will place this crown on his head."
Then: Jesus: "I am waiting to place this crown."
Then: Jesus: shouting: "I am waiting for you Joe!"
Joe standing in the tower window He laughing. He dancing. He Ringing bells!!!!
All eyes on Joe.
Joe: "How you like it, sucker!"
Joe blow Christ off!

## Januuarry (is a year later)

Here is Joe life now He living with Girl and a baby now Is a little Joe but not: is girl: is Baby Girl! She beautiful.

This going be a new adventure.

Often when Joe rocking baby in rocker or singing little songs to, often Joe thinks back to Jimmy acting advice:

Joe remembers what Jimmy say about acting. Knowing person who is his audience. He on stage: stage is life: who in audience? Who playing to?

For Richard J the audience is Pastor Jim: who watching and grimacing and shocked and eyes bugging out as he so offended by Richard J's plays, his words. Joe think Richard J's whole life is a puppet play he performing for this same audience – "now we find Richard Puppet in prison" "OH MY! What a wasted life," shouts Pastor Jim. "Aw go suck it pastor!" says Richard Puppet.

EB sees the doctors who told him son would not live long – his family who tell him to accept this life. "Let it go." "Move on." He sees them in the audience there, in their pews, staring! Leaning waaaaaay back! The power of EB actions blowing them backwards like a terrific wind.

Super Goth maybe see inside in inside of gym teacher mind – this brain cannot accept the Super Goth they see – teacher brain cannot handle at all

Maybe Miguel see the motor he cannot fix. Maybe Old Man see he dead son.

What did Joe see? Who is Joe audience? Is only one. Is Jesus.

Jesus.

All Joe do all Joe life is for Audience of Jesus. Is loving and praising Him.
Then is hating and yelling at.
But all time: it ALL be for Jesus.

When Joe make he terrible faces or scream he terrible things: not truly Jesus who see this: is all of humanity: all around: all see Joe doing these things.

Girl sees. And she loving Joe. Baby Girl loving Joe.

So Joe forgive him. Forgive Sucker JC for blowing him off.

Imagine this:

There Joe at Heaven gates: Joe is shrugging: "Bye Bye Jesus. See you around. Maybe." He tipping he hat (Joe wearing hat) and making a cool salute.

THE END

IS The Temple of
Joe + Girl
and we Baby Girl
Joe + Girl,
All welcome!
Here Our doormat
NO Jesus Allowed!
Go to Hell!
Joe still got it!!!
girl draw

# LAST THING

Dear reader. Thank you for reading and here my parting gift for you.

Try this. Next time you are in a movie theater, and you are watching the great Jimmy Can on the screen. Think this: nothing to worry he is acting, he may seem tough or mean or bad but he not, he is Jimmy

So try this: when Jimmy on big movie screen, say: not in a whisper but not too loud: say: "I'm a friend of Joe!" And guess what you see?

Jimmy will turn and he will smile at you and maybe even wink that Jimmy wink!

# AFTERWORD
# by the author

## My Life With Puppets

Before Joe McPuppet, there was Jim Hill, youth pastor and affable leader of the Christian puppet troupe Puppet2Puppet Puppet Play Productions.

The genesis of both of these characters occurred one super nova of a night in the year 2002—the night I stumbled upon an online database of Christian puppet plays. Usually when a free form internet search serves me up an oddity like this, the impact is ephemeral. But, instead of flashing across my screen, this one stuck.

The site had the handmade quality of a mimeographed Sunday program. Blue text on yellow background, a curly-que font. An internal search engine allowed explorations by subject matter (including helpful categories like "temptation," "second coming," "sharing") presumably for pastors and congregants looking for material to stage in upcoming performances. Titles like "Fruit Of The Spirit Part 1: Love," "God Made The World," and "Christmas Is Coming!"

What, I wondered, would it be like to write a Christian puppet play?

It turned out to be surprisingly easy. And not for the reasons I had guessed. I'd figured that the tools I had accumulated as a working screenwriter with ten years experience writing and revising scripts would guide my hand.

Not so. What made the writing so effortless was the familiarity of the vernacular and the structure—the inevitable movement from shaming towards a simple resolution and message. My church-going days had come to an abrupt stop the moment I left home for college, but years in Sunday School and Youth Group were now paying off.

My first script was **"In The Garden".** I wrote a catchy synopsis: *"Boy Scouts on a camping trip face a biblical dilemma. Or do they? A very special friend helps them sort it all out."*

I uploaded it. By morning, feedback had already been posted.

| **In The Garden** | Rating: **1** |
|---|---|
| UUUUGH! I hated this skit. | |
| | |
| **Blasphemy** | Rating: **1** |
| That was a terrible portrayal of our Lord. He would never say: "let's get it on" or something like "I would vote him off the island." Really guys Jesus is allknowing not a long-lost camping guys. You really riled me up on this one. | |

I was hooked.

So I wrote another. And another. Coming from a family of Methodist ministers (my father, my uncle, my stepfather, his father), I had plenty of material to draw on. And maybe…just maybe…some unresolved questions about faith and belief?

If you were a friend of mine back then, you would have been invited (commanded) to contribute a play to my new collective, Puppet2Puppet Puppet Play Productions. I made the call and they answered it. Soon the list of the database's newest puppet plays were stocked by P2P work. We also dominated the list ranking the top plays by views. Lots and lots of views. Like hundreds. Thousands. Tens of thousands.

This thing was getting bigger than me. I needed someone to steer the ship.

Enter Jim Hill. As a youth pastor with a passionate involvement in his church's puppet program, Jim was just the man for the job. He could do what I couldn't – promote and nurture these precious play with full heart and full throat. He sent weekly online newsletters to the members of the collective, full of lavish praise for our puppet authors' latest works and homey stories about his adopted 19-year-old son Jim Jr (Carl.)

***Isn't it great that God, in His eternal wisdom, made everyone different? How boring would this world be if fish could fly and birds could swim (though it'd be kinda cool to see that! HA!). We at P2P celebrate the diversity of God's creations, and their beliefs.***

***We who call ourselves "Christians" are often seen as outside of the mainstream. Perhaps we are a "counter-culture" like the Hippies of yester-year and folk like the "Goths" of today.***

***Well, mister, I'm happy to call myself a "weirdo" and a "misfit" as long as I can love my neighbor and turn the other cheek and just say "hey, pal, as long as you're okay, I'm okay." (How's ol' Jim doing with the lingo of today?)***

***So go ahead and just call me an old fuzzy so-and-so who needs to lose some weight (You'd be right!) Ask Jim Jr. (Carl).***

***Have a great Thanksgiving!***

Soon Jim was fielding requests for translations of our popular plays and soothing readers who were outraged over the more controversial plays. Like "Adam and Steve," "Every Saturday Night," "Goodbye Gramma," and…

### Just In Case Hugs

**Description:** The importance of hugs, just in case.

| **Wrong Message to Send!** (Rated by: **Anonymous**) Posted September 16 2015 | Rating: **1** |
|---|---|
| We need to teach children to be in relationship with God with their sins forgiven. We do not need to teach them that the worst part of death would be to have not gotten a hug from their mom or dad that day! The worst part of death would be for the person who dies to not know Jesus! | |
| **No Heading** (Rated by: **NotYou**) Posted November 28 2010 | Rating: **5** |
| I would seriously up the age on this script. It's more like 10+ | |

Over time, like with most things, I grew to feel confined by the parameters of the puppet play genre as practiced by P2P, even though I had created those parameters. I longed to write (even more) subversive plays. But I had a problem. I had grown fond of my Pastor Jim and didn't want to upset his pleasant world.

Joe McPuppet was born. Where Jim was ever calm and trusting in his faith, Joe was perpetually angry at his former Savior and the church folk who remained devoted to Him. In short order, Joe kicked out a series of fast-paced stories that were barely plays, more like screeds coming straight from his mind to the page. Automatic writing.

The first was a re-telling of the parable of the prodigal son—with a twist – the father who graciously welcomes home his wayward son turns out to be an axe murderer.

**SARAH**
Hey Choir! Thank you for singing about God and Jesus!

**CHOIR**
"Singing about God and Jesus?" We are singing about Tom's father! We are a cult and believe that Tom's father is God!

**TOM**
I knew it!

**FATHER**
I'm going to kill you!!!!

**SARAH**
Look out, Tom, he has an axe!

**FATHER**
Die, die, die, die!

In "Lazarus," JC is a blowhard who raises an army of dead critics to attack Joe's plays.

**GOOD PEOPLE**
We love you, Lazarus! Entertain us with your words!

**LAZARUS**
You people rule! Here is a thought I just had. What if God loved

EVERYONE?! I'm going to write a play about it.

**GOOD PEOPLE**
Hurray, we can't wait to read it!

**CRITIC**
You can wait!

**The critic has a rifle and shoots Joe.**

**CRITIC**
Die, Lazarus, die!

Joe was on a roll.

Meanwhile, things at Puppet2Puppet took a strange turn – the troupe's plays moved into the real world. It was enough that people were actually performing our plays! Now, ***we*** were performing our plays!

Jim was approached by Penn & Teller's television show *Bullshit!* to perform our play "Up From The Ooze" on an episode of their show debunking stuff they considered BS. Our episode would be about Christians who defied evolution.

DAD: *[lighting a new cigarette]* What else did this teacher tell you?

DAVID: We talked about how the world was born, and *[looking at a piece of paper tucked in his PeeChee]* how life came from the pry-more-dee-ull OOZE. [l*aughs in expectation of his father joining in. There is an uncomfortable silence].* Miss Del Mundo says that the ooze got smarter at getting food and started to multiply and it like turned into a fish or something, and then the fish sort of grew legs only it took a long long time for that to happen, and that's sort of how we got here.

DAD: Go to your room.

We had to turn Penn & Teller's show down cuz we didn't actually have any puppets. But we rectified that little problem before the next opportunity came along. Which was soon…

We paraded our new puppets across the stage of the Key Club on Sunset Blvd in Hollywood as part of Puppet Terror, a punk vaudeville show created by forever LA hipsters Pleasant Gehman and Iris Berry. The play we chose to perform for these leather-clad, skinny-tied sinners was our 9/11-themed "Heaven Needs Firemen."

Heaven Needs Firemen

*This play takes a tough subject (September 11th) and puts it into a Christian context for the kids to understand. [Because the play involves the death of a parent, the ideal age group is kids age 5-9.]*

Jim made a big deal about fifty souls giving themselves to Christ that night, kneeling right there on Sunset Blvd. Personally, I didn't see it.

Stepping so deeply into the real-world role as a puppeteer led to Lifetime Television flying me to Las Vegas. The gig? To film a TV proposal, with a puppet naturally, to my "girlfriend" (perfectly played by fellow P2P puppeteer Sara Vidar). I may have been listed as "Tim Kirk" but I was channeling the affable Jim Hill – blind and deaf to even the most outright ridicule. A treasured memory from this experience was on set, as I watched two grips methodically kicking one another in the shins to stifle their laughter while I performed the fifth take of "will you marry me?" in a high squeaky puppet voice.

| VIDEO: | AUDIO: |
| --- | --- |
| | |
| | |
| | |
| Tim | (TIM)<br>SARAH, YOU'RE THE PUPPETMASTER OF MY HEART. YA TUG AT MY HEARTSTRINGS ... |
| Pics of Tim and Sarah<br>Marry Me Moments gfx | (VO)<br>WHEN PUPPETEER TIM POPPED THE QUESTION TO SARAH ON THE AIR, HE TUGGED AT *VIEWERS*' HEARTSTRINGS. BUT WOULD SHE FEEL THE SAME WAY? |
| | |
| Transition to reaction video | (TIM, OC)<br>... AND NOW, I'VE FINALLY FOUND THE WORDS TO SAY: |
| Tim and Sarah reacting | (TIM, OC)<br>WILL YOU MARRY ME? |
| | |
| Sarah with puppet | "I WILL!" |
| | |
| Tim | "THANKS, LIFETIME!" |

Next up, a puppet adaptation of a Jack Chick religious tract for the film anthology "Hot Chicks."

As cool as all this was, the pinnacle of these experiences had to be, hands down, appearing in a pilot for *America's Next Muppet*, auditioning for the part in front of a panel of Muppet judges: Gonzo, Pepe the King Prawn and the grande dame Miss Piggy.

As I stood behind the curtain clutching my Satan doll, I heard the words that would stir any young puppeteer's heart – Kermit, waving his green hands, and shouting "Ladies and Gentlemen, Tim Kirk and Beezle!!""

Me: Hello everybody. I'm Tim. Let me introduce you to my friend. Say hello to the people.

Satan: *Hell*-lo.

M: C'mon don't be shy, tell 'em your name.

S: I have many names. Some call me Lucifer, some call me Old Scratch, the Prince of Darkness, the Prince of Lies.

M: Well, what should we call you?

S: Call me Beezle…bub!

M: Ouch!

S: What do you want from me, *I'm eeeeevil!*

M: So, Beezle, who's your favorite Muppet?

S: Why Gonzo, of course!

M: Gonzo? Why's that?

S: He's got soul.

M: So you like soul, huh? Soul food, soul music…?

S: No. Just souls!

M: Oh boy. Well, why do you think you'd be a good muppet?

S: I love children.

M: You love children?

S: I love their souls! What do you want from me? *I'm eeeevil!*

Gonzo and Pepe were kind but Ms. Piggy was relentlessly mean. "You worry me," she finished her blistering critique. "Do you live alone?"

"Yes. Well…with my puppet."

"Get him out of here!"

Joe needed a place in the real world too. CHRIST NEVER SHOWED UP landed in the blogsphere in 2003. The weekly, often daily, entries followed Joe's adventures (many of which made their way into this book.) Over the years, like Joe, I held various jobs, met James Caan, watched *Passion of the Christ* (but never *Who's Harry Crumb*), married Girl and had Baby Girl.

And here we are.

In the wrestling world, I am told, there exists a term called "kayfabe." This describes the false drama in the ring—the staged fights and invented rivalries. They don't seem to have a word for the moment when the illusion is dropped, the façade destroyed. When the wrestler yells at his opponent in the ring, "hey dumby, you were supposed to throw the fight."

I guess this book is that. I am pulling back the curtain on Puppet2Puppet to reveal the truth. For twenty years, I have protected these characters and the work they created. I have been reluctant to give up the game. Reluctant to expose that these guys were, well, me!

But I am no longer afraid.

Jim Lives!

Joe Lives!

- Tim Kirk, Los Angeles, October 29th, 2021

Puppet plays cited written by: In the Garden, Adam and Steve – Tim Kirk; Every Saturday Night – David Carpenter; Goodbye Gramma – Todd Hughes; Just In Case Hugs – Mark Givens; The Prodigal Son, Lazarus – Joe McP; Up From The Ooze – Johnny Puppet; Heaven Needs Firemen – Joel Huschle.

# ABOUT THE AUTHOR

Tim Kirk is a writer and filmmaker. He has produced the documentaries *Room 237* and *The El Duce Tapes*, along with a dozen other films including *The Nightmare*, *And With Him Came the West* and *A Glitch in the Matrix.* He also writes and directs indie narrative films, like *Director's Commentary: Terror of Frankenstein*, *The Mystery of Durango* and *Sex Madness Revealed.* He is the author of the multi-generational western novel, *BURNT* and a collection of short stories, *The Feral Boy Who Lives in Griffith Park*, now in a second expanded printing. He lives in Los Angeles with his wife, his daughter, and several puppets.

112 Harvard Ave #65
Claremont, CA 91711 USA
pelekinesis@gmail.com
www.pelekinesis.com
Pelekinesis titles are available through Small Press Distribution, Baker & Taylor, Ingram, Bertrams, and directly from the publisher's website.

www.ingramcontent.com/pod-product-compliance
Lightning Source LLC
Chambersburg PA
CBHW041642010726
47507CB00012B/431

* 9 7 8 1 9 4 9 7 9 0 5 6 6 *